D0512543

BRODIE McHAGGIS

Other books by Helen Campbell

Brodie McHaggis and the Secret of Loch Ness
ISBN: 978-0-9551386-0-7

BRODIE McHAGGIS

AND THE CURSE OF THE SCOTCH MIST

Helen Campbell

Chloe Publishing

All rights reserved; no part of this publication may be reproduced or transmitted by any means, electronic, mechanical, photocopying or otherwise, without the prior permission of the Publisher

First published in Great Britain in 2007
by Chloe Publishing Ltd, Halkirk, Caithness, KW12 6YJ, Scotland

Copyright © Helen Campbell, 2007

Helen Campbell has asserted her moral rights

A CIP catalogue record of this book is available from the British Library

Cover illustrations by Kimi Rea. Copyright © Helen Campbell 2007
Brodie McHaggis, names, characters and related indicia are copyright
© Helen Campbell 2007

ISBN 978-0-9551386-1-4

Printed, typeset and bound in Great Britain by
Highland Printers, Inverness, Scotland

First Edition 2007

www.hcampbell.com
www.chloepublishing.com
www.brodiemchaggis.com

To

Ishbel, Kathleen and Claire for providing me with the encouragement to finish writing this book

To

Brodie's fans

Thank you
x

Can you see into the other world . . .

. . . the world that most of us are too busy to notice?

PROLOGUE

The Haggis

The haggis is an odd-looking creature. Newly born haggises, or haggisen, could be mistaken for ginger-red cotton wool balls running around on three matchsticks. Their ability to run and swim with only three legs, and use their feet as hands and fingers too, is both comical and astounding. They love to sing and their bagpipe wails can be heard for miles around. Seeing the haggis at work and at play is both an incredible and inspiring sight to watch.

Unfortunately, Brodie McHaggis may have changed all of that. It may only be a matter of time before there will be no more haggises to watch; no more haggises to run around the Dunroamin hillside; and no more haggises to listen to.

In his belief that he has freed the haggises from all danger, Brodie was only too happy to return home after his battles with his darkest enemy, Gertruda McNorris. But he is just about to discover how wrong he was and how close he is to a world without haggises. The battle continues …

CHAPTER ONE

Home, Sweet Home

The yellow January moon shone boldly, lighting up the small picturesque village of Drumdrui and the wintry rowan trees guarding each of the haggis burrows like Highland soldiers. The night was calm and peaceful, apart from the sound of snoring haggises in their burrows. It was so good to be back home. Brodie had missed everything about it – even the pranks from Iron McGillis, the smells from Saunders McRancid and having to look after the haggisen in The Bothy. There was no place like home, sweet home.

The sound of rustling leaves blowing in the wind caused Brodie some concern and he looked up at the rowan trees. He stared blankly at them as the moonlight cast their leafless shadows onto the snow-covered ground. There were no leaves – and there was no wind. Brodie's blood turned to ice as he realised what he had done. The sound of rustling leaves continued. It meant only one thing – danger was close by and the dryads were warning him.

Only a short time ago he had left the shores of Loch Ness with the biggest feeling of pride that he had ever felt. He was proud that he had conquered their darkest enemy – that he had done it by himself – without his father's help. He had been heartbroken to leave Erin behind in the Highlands – a new experience to him for it was the first time he had ever had to leave a friend, knowing that he would never see her again. He could still see the sadness on Erin's face as he was whisked away by Nessie and Petula. He had felt somewhat guilty at being so pleased to be going home when he knew that she would miss him so much. So pleased to be able to see his mother and father again. His friends. And Kyla McHarris. His heart skipped a pleasant beat at the thought of Kyla.

The sound of rustling leaves grew stronger. Brodie's heart

jumped around in his chest as he fought with his fears. He looked down at the piece of wart-encrusted heather, pinned to the fine plait tied tightly around his ankle. He remembered when Erin had pressed the safety-pin through the heather. It was faint – but distinct. A woman's scream. It had been Gertruda's scream. She was still alive! Brodie's stomach dropped like lead. He had to return. He had to take Gertruda back to the Highlands. A wave of panic washed through his small, fur-covered body as he realised that he had brought danger to everyone.

He thought that he had won the battle – but Gertruda had won, this time. She had goaded him into reducing her to heather. Into taking her back to Drumdrui as a trophy. She had used him. The goblins and boglouts had been a part of it as well. The more they had pushed to get her back, the more determined Brodie had been to take her back to Drumdrui. Just what she had wanted.

It now felt as though a gale-force wind was blowing through the trees as the sound of rustling leaves became deafening. The dryads were warning Brodie that the danger was getting closer. That Gertruda was about to join them.

Brodie suddenly felt himself being catapulted into the air at high speed. The blood rushed to his head and his eyes strained as he dangled in the air by one of his ankles. The ankle with the plait around it.

'Well, well, well young Brodie McHaggis. Fancy you taking me home to meet your parents. I take it we are at home? Tell me … where is home … where are we …?'

All Brodie could see was the black, grimy, moth-eaten cloth that his face was buried in. It smelt old and musty. His feet went cold and numb as the blood continued to rush to his head.

Gertruda McNorris's crackly voice was very distinct. 'I'll get that little wretch of a girl for piercing my nose with this pin,' she howled as Brodie's weight pulled down on her head. 'Almost gave myself away when I screamed,' she tutted, gripping her hands around

Brodie's body and lifting him up so that she could see him.

Her old blood-shot eyes were full of hatred. Red circles formed around her piercing black pupils. Her grey cracked lips parted to reveal a mouth of rotting teeth. Brodie coughed violently as the acrid smell from her mouth burned at his lungs.

'Bye-bye, wee furry beastie. It's been such a delight knowing you! Shame we didn't manage to spend much time together, but … well, at least we can say we were quite close in the end, ha, ha, ha!'

Gertruda's cackle shuddered through Brodie's veins. His fear and worry was suddenly overcome by rage. He had to get rid of her before she could raise a spell. He simply had to.

Gertruda lifted him higher so that they were eyeball to eyeball. He was losing feeling in his body and he was becoming faint.

'Still can't believe how strange you creatures are,' Gertruda muttered childishly as she examined him closely. She angled her head from one side and then to the other side, smiled girlishly, frowned a little, then paused before straightening her head and pressing her face right into Brodie's face.

'And don't even think about using the Silent Protector that Noremac blessed you with. I came willingly – I got inside the spell and on my journey here … wherever here is,' she whispered, glancing around the dark night, 'and I broke the code! Well, Noremac.' She rolled her head back and laughed into the night air. 'You didn't think that I would suss that spell out now, did you?!!.'

Brodie's anger almost burst a blood vessel in his head as he tried and tried to use the Silent Protector on the witch, but he failed miserably. Nothing happened and he finally gave in to exhaustion.

All of a sudden, Gertruda's eyes shot up to the top of their bony sockets and her mouth opened widely as though she was in pain. A green glow formed at the back of her throat and steam began to puff out of it. Then steam puffed out of her ears and nose.

The noise of rustling leaves continued to whip around the dark night, almost piercing Brodie's eardrums. Gertruda's grip around him loosened and he fell to the ground, landing face first in the snow.

He lay still for a few moments, slightly concussed. His nose and head throbbed. He listened. Everything around him had gone quiet. Staggering to his feet, Brodie regained his balance.

'Brodie. You must go – now,' said a soothing, female voice from above him.

'Huh?'

'Go now – and take Gertruda with you. Quickly!' She spoke with urgency.

Brodie looked down at the ground and noticed the wart-infested heather hanging, once again, from the plait around his leathery ankle. He lifted his leg and examined it closely. The heather moved – like a beating heart. It was getting stronger by the beat. He looked at the trees above him. The rustling had stopped.

'How … who?'

A number of small brown eyes blinked from the bark on each tree. Dryads.

'But she said the Silent Protector wouldn't work. Gertruda said that she knew the code and that I couldn't use it on her again.'

Brodie peered hard into the trees until one of the dryads revealed herself, her skin camouflaging her well against the bark. The nymph-like dryad climbed slowly down the tree trunk on her hands and feet, like a wild cat on its haunches. She had green tinged hair. Her translucent wings flapped slightly as she cocked her head from side to side, listening through her knotty ears. Her long and pointed face was full of anger and her brown eyes were sharp. She didn't show the friendliness of the dryad in the forest, but she spoke with the same warmth.

'Brodie – you have brought danger to Drumdrui. We have never seen such a strong witch before. We have never had to reveal ourselves to you before.'

Brodie nodded in agreement. He hadn't seen a dryad until he was in the forest with Erin. They had told him how they only revealed themselves in times of danger.

'As Gertruda gets closer to fulfilling her vow, she will get even stronger. You must take her away – quickly. It won't be long before she is back.' The dryad pushed her long pointed face forward and stared hard into Brodie's crystal-blue eyes. He watched her turn around in a semi-circle and climb back up the tree trunk. She leant over a branch to speak to him.

'Witches do not normally come near us – but Gertruda had no choice. You brought her here. We,' she paused to look around at the other trees cautiously, 'helped to drain her energy. The others used the Silent Protector on her. Most of them have not had to use it before. None of them know that they possess it.

'Gertruda did not go voluntary this time, so who knows how she will come out of this one. Each haggis has an individual code, which Gertruda will have to unlock to get out of the spell without turning into your friend. It may take her a little longer to unlock so many – but we sense her determination. She will come back – but because she did not go voluntary, the others should be safe, for now – they should still be able to use the Silent Protector on her. You, on the other hand, are not so lucky. You have to get her back to where she came from – NOW!' The dryad hissed deeply and merged back into the branch before Brodie could answer her.

'I'm sorry. Really, I am. Please dryad, don't be angry with me.' He waited for a reply, but there was nothing. His eyes widened. 'I'll sing for you,' but no reply came back. He hung his head low between his shoulders and sighed deeply, muttering and snivelling to himself. He was too young to have these pressures. He didn't know what to do. What did the dryad mean the others? What others?

A loud familiar sound of heavily snoring haggises broke

Brodie's thoughts. He raised his head and looked around the burrows.

'Huh?'

His eyes widened with surprise. Every haggis had come out of their burrows and had unknowingly used the Silent Protector on Gertruda. Mirg McVey, Stan McGillis, Vanora McTavish, Angus McMail, Hamish McTosh, Macca McRoberts. Everyone. Oh, he really was in big trouble now. How was he going to explain this one?

Then he remembered what the dryad had said and sighed with relief. Not one of them would remember it when they woke up. It was part of the Silent Protector. A part that Erin had helped him to remember. He looked over at the McHaggis burrow to catch a glimpse of his parents before he left for the Highlands again – but they were nowhere to be seen. His heart ached. Where were they?

Tears blinded Brodie and snow began to fall as he sped through the heathery hills towards Darmaeddie Loch. He had no time to lose. He had to get Gertruda back to the forest and quickly. Without giving another thought to the dangerous Kelpie who lived in the loch, Brodie splashed clumsily into the icy water. It stabbed at his skin and eventually numbed his body, but he swam on as fast as he could. Gertruda could appear at any time now and on his own, he could do nothing to stop her.

CHAPTER TWO

The Untuned Melody

The swim to the Rainbow Cave seemed to take an eternity. Brodie bobbed around in the icy water, waiting for a plesiosaur to open the entrance to the cave – the entrance to the Secret of Loch Ness.

The tension throbbed in his head as he waited, and waited, and waited. He shivered with cold and fear. Fear that Gertruda would soon break the spell. Fear that she would wreak havoc through the Dunroamin hillside. All because of his selfish need to find out the truth behind the myths. If only he could go back to the way it was. The way he used to stand at the loch side asking his father question after question about the myths. As much as he had hated his father getting angry about the questions, he would give anything to have that back. Anything.

Brodie's legs grew tired so he swam to the shore for a rest. After he had regained his breath and stopped wheezing, he cleared his airways and rotated his head 360 degrees on his neck, snapping it back like an elastic band. He fanned his nostrils and began to sing like he'd never sung before. Only this time, his song wasn't like the choir of angels playing bagpipes. It was full of panic and fear. It was troubled – fast, tuneless and emotional.

Brodie's twenty-four toe-like fingers continued pressing along his nose and nostrils to change the pitch of the notes. The sound was awful, but it was all that he could manage. His throat hurt. His head thumped, and his heart beat faster than he ever thought it could.

'Ok. Ok. OK! Give us a break, why don't you? Didn't we send you home, never to come back here again?'

Brodie tumbled over backwards and crashed into a snow-covered shrub after rolling a few times. The snow slid from the shrub and landed all over him.

'Will you stop fooling around and tell me why you're still here?' Ranald, one of the smaller plesiosaurs that Brodie had met earlier in the Rainbow Cave, waited for Brodie's explanation.

Brodie picked himself up, brushed the snow from his fur and quickly tripled across to the water's edge where he stared right into the creature's green, football-sized eyes. They widened as Brodie unfolded the truth about Gertruda. Ranald backed away from Brodie and stared at the pulsing heather hanging from his ankle.

'Please, don't go! I need you to take me back. Don't you see? We are all in danger here.'

'And it's all because of a medalling little haggis.' Ranald watched the heather as it beat continuously like a heart. 'How long have we got?'

'Not long,' replied Brodie hurriedly. 'We have to go now.'

'Hurry then. Stay close – I'll take you through.' Ranald was far from pleased. He was taking danger into their sanctuary and he knew that Nessie would be very angry with him, but what was worse? That, or leaving Gertruda to take her revenge on the haggis?

Brodie splashed into the dark, icy water and followed the plesiosaur as he glided effortlessly towards the rock face. Just as his scaly nose was an inch from it, the rock face opened and a bright flash of rainbow light lit up the water, almost blinding Brodie. He tucked himself in close by Ranald's giant fin and when the tip of Ranald's long, scaly tail was inside the Rainbow tunnel, the rock face snapped shut.

'So, what was that horrendous noise out there?' asked Petula, quizzically circling Ranald in the Rainbow Cave. A questioning silence fell as dozens of pairs of football-sized eyes bore down on the young plesiosaur. Water dripping from the rainbow-coloured stalactites splashed loudly onto the marble floor, causing them all to turn their gaze to the back of the cave briefly, and then back to

Ranald for an explanation.

Brodie could see the seven different tunnels where the rainbow-coloured light was coming from. Just below the surface of the water – red and orange tunnels pulsed brightly; a sparkling yellow tunnel, and green, blue, violet and indigo tunnels all flickered giving the cave its wonderful coloured effect. He swam to the side and clumsily struggled out of the water onto the marble floor. His breathless wheezing echoed around the cave like deflating bagpipes.

'Brodie?!' cried the plesiosaurs in unison.

Brodie drew himself up to his full height of just eighteen inches and froze to the spot. He eventually plucked up the courage to turn his head back towards them and was met by two large flared nostrils. Nessie's nostrils.

'Are you the cause of that noise out there? It was absolutely horrid. Tell me, quickly, young haggis.' Nessie snapped her teeth and tugged at some of Brodie's wet fur.

'Y-y-yes. It was m-m-me,' he stuttered as he watched Nessie's large teeth reflect the bright colours of the cave.

'But, what on earth for? Goodness me – didn't we just take you back to the shores of Darmaeddie Loch? Didn't we make sure that you got there safely? What are you doing back here? And so ssssoon?' Nessie emphasised her last word as she nudged him with her wet scaly nose.

'I have to go back to Loch Ness. I have to go now. We're all in danger!' Brodie looked down at the piece of heather as it continued to pulsate, getting stronger by the minute, and he hurriedly explained what had happened at Drumdrui. Nessie stared long and hard at the heather before answering him.

'Quickly. Get it off your foot. I'll take it myself and leave it in the loch.'

'Do you hear that?' said Nessie's friend, Petula.

The plesiosaurs bent their heads towards the green tunnel leading from the Rainbow Cave and listened. Brodie listened too.

There was no mistaking the angelic sounds of a haggis singing. It sounded just like Brodie at the shores of Loch Ness two hours before as he called for Nessie.

'I don't understand. There shouldn't be any haggises at Loch Ness!' Nessie's eyes grew concerned, then angry. 'Not another meddling haggis! How did that one slip by us? This is the last – we can't risk our own lives any more. The last – you hear me Brodie McTrouble. The absolute last time!'

Brodie blinked hard at every word that Nessie fired at him. She was really angry.

'Never mind taking the heather off. You're coming with me!' Without another word, she gestured to him to climb into the rope net lying in the corner of the cave. The same net he had been taken home in. He did as he was instructed and fed the rope net into her jaws. She gripped it between her large teeth and whisked him into the water and through the spangly green tunnel. He had never been so afraid.

Petula swam close to Nessie and gripped the other end of the net. They were taking no chances this time – nobody was going to take Brodie from them when they got to Loch Ness.

The journey seemed to take much longer than it had before. Much, much longer. The heather pulsed stronger against Brodie's ankle. He willed Nessie to go faster.

CHAPTER THREE

The Enemy Approaches

Erin stood frozen with horror, her eyes fixed on the moss-speckled heather pinned to Dion Cameron's white tartan dress. The hair prickled across her skin as she listened to the Canadian singer's voice echo mystically around the ruins of Urquhart Castle to the tunes of Auld Lang Syne. The guests were dotted around the wintry castle grounds, singing along with her.

Dion brushed the heather with her slim hand, smiled and then winked at Erin as she continued to sing. "It will bring me luck," she had said as Erin had reluctantly given it to her. The only luck that the white heather brought was to haggises. She knew that the heather was once Brodie's enemy – the moss-eaten, vicious little ghillie dhu. She knew that soon, very soon, the spell would wear off and the ghillie dhu would be dangling from her dress rather than a piece of beautiful, unusually moss-speckled, lucky white heather.

Erin pulled her father's black coat around her green tartan skirt and jacket and slipped away from the celebrations, walking over the bridge and away from the castle ruins. When she was sure that nobody could see her, she ran as fast as her sandal-clad feet would carry her. The ice bit at her toes, but she ran on. She had to warn Brodie. Somehow, she had to.

***

The smooth, dark surface of Loch Ness broke quietly as the plesiosaurs surfaced with Brodie. They stayed low and glided elegantly towards the shore just below Urquhart Castle. The faint sound of people singing and laughing filtered to the shore. The pale red and green glows of the Northern Lights pulsed gently through the crisp, night sky. It was calm and peaceful. Peaceful, even with the melodic sounds of the haggis singing.

'It sounds just like you, Brodie,' Nessie whispered as she and Petula glided slowly and quietly in towards the shore, their large heads barely out of the water.

Brodie listened to the music. He had to agree, it did sound like him. He was still in the net, but was now swimming with the plesiosaurs rather than being dragged by them. He could just make out an outline of something on the shore.

The haggis continued to sing.

They all moved in closer. Closer. Closer still.

The singing stopped abruptly. There was a clicking noise for a number of seconds, and then it started again. Just the same as before. Just like Brodie.

'Recognise who it is Brodie?'

Brodie squinted his large round eyes, but he just couldn't make out a haggis. He felt a hard tug at his ankle. His fur bristled and his heart skipped another beat.

'Nessie! We have to hurry. It's Gertruda. She's getting stronger!'

Cold water splashed into Brodie's face as Nessie and Petula picked up speed and dragged him with them. He coughed and spluttered, almost choking on the water as it was forced into his mouth and down his throat.

The haggis singing stopped. There was sudden movement on the shore. Nessie and Petula stopped and listened.

'Nessie?' The female voice came from the shore.

Brodie's heart jumped.

'Erin?'

'Brodie!' Relief flowed through Erin's body as she heard Brodie's voice. She peered through the darkness until she saw the shiny scales on Nessie's skin. Petula stayed in the background, afraid to show herself.

'I have to warn you – about Gertruda. She tricked you.'

Nessie released the net and Brodie splashed clumsily to the shore. He was numb with cold. His legs lost their feeling and became entangled in one another. He slumped to the ground like a wet rag. Every time he tried to get up, he fell back down again. His legs just wouldn't obey what his brain was asking them to do; they were like rubber.

Erin stood and giggled. It was a shame to laugh at him, but he did look funny.

Brodie hated being laughed at and he lost his temper. 'Stop laughing and help me will you? Quickly! Take her away from me. She's already been back. She's got my code. I can't use the Silent Protector against her again. Quick!' Brodie pointed to his ankle as though it was on fire.

Puzzled by Brodie's ramblings, Erin rushed to his aid. She fumbled for the safety pin, released the heather from Brodie's ankle and threw it to the ground. The warts on the heather had grown larger and pulsed even harder.

'We need to get her back to the forest – and quick,' said Brodie through sharp breaths. Time was quickly running out. Gertruda would soon be with them again – free of the forest – and free to hunt the haggis.

Nessie rose from the water and tilted her smooth head to the night sky. Water dripped from her skin into the loch as a high-pitched scream curled from her mouth. Brodie immediately plugged his ears – the scream was so piercing it was painful, but to the untrained ear her cries for help were barely noticeable.

Erin frowned at the tortured look on Brodie's face. Then she looked to Nessie and watched as the plesiosaur looked to be calling for someone. Erin listened hard. She heard a faint noise – like a girl screaming – far, far in the distance. It was so faint, that she wasn't sure if she even heard anything. Almost immediately, two large tawny owls flew from what seemed to be out of nowhere and perched in the tree beside them.

'Thank you for coming so quickly.' Nessie spoke hurriedly. 'I have bad news – the enemy approaches. I want you take that piece of white heather back to Gertruda's forest and drop it right into the centre. Make sure it goes into the forest and doesn't get stuck at the top of a tree. Be quick – and be careful. It will be a danger to us all if we don't get it back there.'

The owls knew that Nessie's cries for help were urgent and desperate. With a small hoot and a twist of his head, the largest owl swooped down to the shore, grasped the heather in his claws and soared into the sky. The smaller owl hooted, spread her wings and joined her partner as they flew across the loch effortlessly. Erin watched their peaceful silhouettes fly across the moon before they veered towards the forest, eventually swallowed up by the velvety darkness.

The numbness had finally gone from Brodie's legs and he managed to stand up, feeling slightly shaky. 'Where's the other haggis?' he asked tripling up and down the small shore like a guard dog. 'Where is he?' He sounded challenging.

Erin looked puzzled.

'I heard him singing. Where is he?'

Erin laughed warmly. 'No, silly. I recorded you on my camcorder. I was just playing it back so that I could get a message to you – through Nessie.'

'Recorded? Play back? What are you talking about?' Brodie was puzzled and frowned heavily at Erin.

Nessie raised her head out of the water, momentarily. 'Those new-fangled machines,' she hissed. 'They are going to be the death of us yet. We're being hunted daily by men with stupid machines! Get rid of it Erin. You must get rid of it. They can't find us. They simply can't!' Nessie's voice was full of panic.

'Erin? What are you doing down here? Your father is looking for you. We're all heading back up to the main building.'

Erin swung around. Harold Gunn's large silhouetted frame stood at the top of the steps.

Brodie's body shuddered at the sound of the butcher's deep voice and he sneaked into Erin's rucksack to hide.

'Oh – just looking,' she replied nervously, wondering how much Harold Gunn had seen and heard.

'Ach lass – you won't find Nessie tonight – it's too bright and cold. You'll never see her when the Northern Lights are out.'

Erin almost coughed a laugh. That was the only time that Nessie thought it was safe to surface. When everyone was much too interested in the lights in the sky. Her theory was that they wouldn't be looking at the loch. They wouldn't be looking for her.

'Anyway – your folks are looking for you. Best make your way back.' Harold leant on the gate at the top of the steps as he waited for Erin.

Erin reached for her rucksack. Brodie was curled up inside, looking like a hunted animal again. She picked up her camera and stuffed it in the side pocket of the rucksack. There was no way she was erasing Brodie's song or the pictures that she had taken of him and Nessie. She would find a safe place for them.

Harold Gunn began to walk down the steps towards her. Erin couldn't risk him seeing Nessie, so she ran up the steps towards him. 'It's alright, I'm on my way – no need to come down Mr Gunn.'

'Strange place for a young girl of your age to hang out. Aren't you scared down here?'

'Now Mr Gunn. Don't try any of those scary stories with me. If I was scared – do you really think I'd be down here alone? And as for Nessie – well, I'm not looking for her. She doesn't exist. As if I'd believe in any of that anyway. Pah!' Erin turned away from him and pulled the rucksack over her shoulders, hoping she sounded convincing.

The large butcher chuckled heartily. 'So you say, Erin. So

you say. Just like haggises, eh? They don't exist.' He continued to chuckle as they climbed the stairs back up towards the party.

Erin looked over her shoulder towards the loch. It was as smooth as black glass. Nessie was gone. How was she going to get Brodie back home now?

Just two days ago, Erin would never have believed that haggises existed. Or that another world ran along side her own world – oblivious to most. She had entered their world through no fault of her own, and now she couldn't seem to get out of it.

She had battled with Gertruda; with the moss-ridden ghillie dhu; with her neighbour's wide-eyed gnome; and she had helped Brodie to fight off goblins, boglouts and … the little red-handed solider, Ly Erg. Erin wanted everything to be like it was at the beginning of the week. She wanted to be able to forget everything that had happened. Even that haggises actually existed, but she could never really forget Brodie. He was the most unusual, most exciting thing that had ever happened to her. She bent down and rubbed her bruised shin, smiling faintly. Brodie had kicked her just before he had left Loch Ness for home. Yes, he was most certainly real and she would never be able to forget him.

She pulled her father's warm coat around her and slid her hand into the pocket, knocking the piece of red porcelain that she had picked off the snow earlier. It was all that was left of the red-handed soldier who had threatened Brodie that he would die if he did not give him the heather – Gertruda. Although at that time, they had thought Gertruda would be a piece of heather forever – a trophy of the war between her and the haggises. Brodie hadn't wanted to give up his trophy so he had disposed of the soldier in a most unusual way with his powerful haggis smell – the haggises' defence against the deadly Highland midge.

Erin recalled the soldier's stern words. "*I am Ly Erg – an omen of death. Challenge me and you'll die within a fortnight. Work with me and you will have a second chance.*" Brodie hadn't even made it past the first hour when trouble had struck again. Gertruda had tricked her way through the Secret of Loch Ness and back to the village of Drumdrui, the home of the haggis. Would she remember how she got there? Would she remember the Rainbow Cave – and Nessie? Erin sighed with temporary relief at the thought of the owls delivering the old witch to the forest. Maybe Ly Erg would take back his curse now. Maybe, just maybe Brodie would be safe.

CHAPTER FOUR

The Lucky White Heather

'Are you ok there lass?'

Erin looked up into the butcher's beaming face. As much as she was wary of his intentions, he had always been good to her. Like now. Always taking an interest. Always happy about life. His gold filling glinted and his ruddy cheeks glowed like the embers in a fire. He chuckled again and patted his large stomach with his hands.

Erin mustered a smile.

Brodie breathed shallowly as he listened to their conversation from inside the dark rucksack. Where was she taking him now? He had to go back with Nessie. His heart sank as he remembered Nessie's words. It would be the last time she would risk her life for any haggis. Brodie's limbs ached badly. He was cold and tired. The soft motion of the rucksack had the same effect of a baby being rocked in its cradle. His lids drew down heavily over his eyes and he drifted into an exhausted sleep.

A cold shudder ran through Erin as she and Harold Gunn passed by the trees on their way to rejoin the Burns Supper celebrations. She got the distinct feeling that she was being watched. She paused briefly and stared into the trees, but shook her head dismissively at even thinking that she saw Gertruda in there wearing her hooded cloak. All this faerie world stuff was messing with her mind – she needed some rest.

The mist had quickly rolled in across the loch, snuffing out any signs of water. The air became ghostly quiet as nothing but mist was visible. It had followed Erin up the steps as quickly as she had climbed them. The bright floodlights on the main building up on the hill quickly faded as they too were drowned in mist. Erin became disorientated and soon lost her bearings.

'Can you see through this stuff Mr Gunn?'

'No lass. However, if we keep going straight, we'll be back at the party before you can say boo to a haggis.' Harold's four chins, one folded on top of the other like a roman blind, glistened with droplets of mist as he chuckled mischievously. 'You never know what's going to come out of the mist at you.' His ruddy-coloured face was like a beacon as it beamed back at Erin through the wisps of mist.

Erin rolled her eyes at the butcher and replied to him in a very serious and mature voice. 'It's simple Mr Gunn. There is nothing ghostly about the mist. It's all about the thermocline and the exchange of heat causing the mist to rise from the water. That's all.'

The butcher rubbed at one of his chins with his large hand, still chuckling at Erin. 'Is there nothing you're scared of lass? Huh? Well, the mist is rolling in – it doesn't look like any thermocline to me. I've never seen anything like it … for a while anyway …' His voice trailed off to a long and deep thought.

Erin saw a flash of panic in his usually sparkly eyes. They walked on in silence, following the noise of laughter through the mist back to the main building.

'Erin – I would love for you to introduce me to some of those celebrities in there. What do you reckon? Especially Dion Cameron.' Harold rested his hand on Erin's small shoulder and she almost collapsed under his weight. Her stomach gurgled as she remembered Dion and the piece of moss-speckled heather.

'Tell you what,' she challenged. 'If I introduce you to her, can you try and get that piece of … lucky white heather from her? The piece on her dress. Tell her that you'd like it as a souvenir.'

Harold looked a bit perplexed as they climbed up the last few steps towards the patio. Scottish music was blasting out of the open patio doors and very well-dressed people were being swished around inside to the sounds of the Scottish dance, Strip the Willow.

'Don't ask why,' Erin said firmly. 'Just do it for me – and

I'll introduce you to him there as well.' She pointed to the tall, handsome man that her mother had blushed at when he had spoken to her earlier. Erin felt that his face was vaguely familiar, but she didn't know who he was.

'You mean Eric Duvall? The A-list actor from the movie *The Hunter's Diary*? Wow Erin – you're on!' Harold's cheeks seemed to glow even hotter at the excitement of meeting the celebrities. He was like a child seeing presents under the Christmas tree for the first time on Christmas morning.

Eric turned towards them, holding a heavy crystal glass in one hand. His warm breath curled into a fine mist as he spoke.

'There you are. We all thought you'd got lost in this mist. What have you been up to?' Eric smiled warmly and looked into Erin's young face. She was covered in droplets of mist and her skin was tinged blue with the cold. He placed his hand gently around Erin's waist ushering her inside the warm and cosy building.

'Er ...,' said Erin blushing into the man's handsomely tanned face. She looked down at her sandal-clad feet, which were also turning blue with trudging through the snow. 'Er ...' she looked back at Harold Gunn's eager face. 'I would like to introduce you to our ... er ... haggis catcher – Harold Gunn.'

The tanned skin around Eric's eyes crinkled gently as he smiled even wider and held out his hand to Harold Gunn.

'So,' he began in a soft American accent, 'tell me about this haggis hunting thing ... can I come on your next shoot?'

Harold's face creased into sinful laughter as he extended his shovel-sized hand to shake the actor's hand.

Brodie awoke to the sound of the butcher's laughter and quickly plugged his ears before he was forced to turn him into a clump of heather.

Erin felt Brodie stir in the rucksack. She looked through the doorway and spied her mother at the far side of the hall chatting to guests. After making her excuses to the two men, she made her way towards her mother to ask if they could leave and go home.

'Beats me what you carry around in that bag, Erin,' laughed Harold as she passed by him. He tugged on the rucksack sharply.

Erin pulled away.

'Thanks for the introduction,' he whispered winking at her. 'I owe you one,' he mouthed.

Erin shuddered and weaved her way through the guests.

'For goodness sake Erin – what do you look like? Your hair is almost frozen and your feet look as though they've got frostbite. At least you've got your father's coat on – heaven knows why you'd want to be down at the loch in this weather.'

She nodded silently as her mother continued to lecture her about the importance of staying warm. She didn't feel cold – she had too much to think about. Her mother's lecturing voice faded into the background as she wondered how on earth she was going to get Brodie back to his home, and safely this time.

'You know, you've missed Daniel Radcliffe. He's gone home now. I loved his haggis sporran – how novel! What a lovely boy he is, Erin.'

Erin had to admit she was disappointed that her Harry Potter star had gone. She couldn't even attempt to get his autograph earlier for fear of Brodie reducing him to heather if he noticed the haggis sporran that he was wearing. It was so real looking, but so dead.

Brenda looked around the hall with a smile of success spread across her face. Apart from the incidents at the meal tables earlier, everything else had gone smoothly. All of the guests had been so pleased with the Burns Supper and apparently the incident at dinner had made it even more memorable.

Before the guests left and poured themselves into their limousines and taxis, they rushed up to Brenda and showered her with hugs and kisses telling her they wanted to come back again next year and pleaded with her to put their names on the list for tickets.

Ritchie McTouey waved to Brenda and Erin as he left the

hall, looking somewhat flushed and unsteady. 'Great night Brenda – cannae wait till next year!' he yelled as he staggered his way along the corridor and up the spiral stairs.

Erin was so relieved when her mother finally called for a taxi. At long last they could go home. She was tired. It had been a very long evening and she was desperate to talk to Brodie about what had happened back at Drumdrui.

Dion Cameron's white dress flowed behind her as she rushed over to Erin. 'Where did you say that you got that haggis from? Can I see it again – it was so cute.'

Erin looked around sharply to see if her mother had heard. 'Er, when I was down at the loch earlier, it fell in. I couldn't reach it – silly me. There weren't many made, so you may not find another one. You can try the shops in Drumnadrochit – if they don't have one, then I doubt that anybody will.' Erin smiled sweetly at the beautiful Canadian woman and then gazed down at the piece of moss-speckled heather pinned to her dress.

Dion followed her gaze. 'Oooh – thank you for this heather. It brought me so much luck when I was up there singing. It's so cold and I was sure my voice would dry up.'

'You're welcome.' Erin hesitated. 'I was wondering … could I take it as a souvenir? She picked up a napkin from the table beside her. 'If you sign this and dedicate the heather to me, I could keep it forever.' She opened her father's coat and pulled out a silver pen.

Dion smiled sweetly at the red-haired girl. 'Why of course you can have it honey – if you still had that haggis, why, I would have asked you to swap it with me – shame.'

Brodie awoke to the sounds of her voice and watched carefully through the mesh panel in the rucksack. He drifted into a giddy pleasure as he saw white mist surround Dion and he heard Noremac's soothing voice. 'Brodie – we will get through this together – you'll see. If you keep your strength, then I can keep mine. Keep believing …'

Erin shook the rucksack sharply when she heard Brodie begin to snore. Dion's warm eyes flicked to the rucksack and then back to Erin's ashen face.

'Everything ok?' she asked coolly.

'No … I mean. Yes. Everything is just fine.' Erin quickly thanked Dion Cameron for the heather and put it in her father's coat pocket, promising to try to find her one of 'those haggises' and send it to her. She would dump the heather in the bin before leaving the castle.

'Your mother has my email address,' she shouted back to Erin in her soft-Canadian accent. 'Keep in touch.' Her voice sung the last word across the hall to Erin.

'What do you need her email address for?' Brenda asked her harassed looking daughter.

'She wants me to email and tell her all about the Highland myths and legends,' Erin replied matter-of-factly as if it was an everyday occasion that a famous singer asked you to email them.

'Wow, Erin. You must have made some impression on her. My daughter emailing Dion Cameron. Keep in there girl – I want an invite to her mansion!' Excitement gushed through Brenda at the thought of spending a week in Canada and she flitted off to speak to Ralph.

Erin shrugged her shoulders and headed for the doorway.

'Taxi for the Scotts!' A medium-built man wearing a brown and cream Shetland pullover and brown corduroy trousers stood at the doorway in front of Erin. It was the same man who had driven them to Urquhart Castle and who had tried to frighten her about the mist – just like Harold Gunn had. Grown-ups! As if. They carried on worse than kids. She studied the man for some moments as he scoured the hall looking for them. He smiled shrewdly at her when his eyes locked with hers.

'Ah – there's one of them. The Scott that doesn't believe in the bogie men who hide in the Scotch Mist. Remind me what you were saying about the thermocline. If the mist is all about the thermocline, then what makes it work over ground? Huh? There's plenty of mist rolling around out there on the road and there's not an ounce of water in sight.'

Erin looked at the man's freckle-speckled nose and counted the lines around his smiling eyes as she carefully prepared her response. 'Well …'

'Well stop trying to frighten my child or I'll report you to your boss!' said Brenda tartly as she placed her hands protectively around Erin's shoulders. She pushed past him and Ralph followed closely behind her. Ralph raised his eyebrows and shrugged his shoulders at the taxi driver, who grinned back at him.

They climbed the large spiral staircase and exited the building into the frosty night. The taxi was barely visible through the mist. The taxi driver strode past them and opened the car door for Brenda. She slid graciously onto the leather seat, lifted both of her feet into the car and tucked them behind the seat in front of her as if they were glued together. The taxi driver smiled at Brenda's effortless posture and closed the door gently. He ran around to the other side of the car and did the same for Erin, only she tucked the rucksack in behind the seat in front of her.

After everyone was in and all seatbelts were fastened, the taxi driver steered the car out of the car park and onto the main road. The indicator ticked loudly.

'Don't know why I bothered indicating. Nobody can see through this mist. It's like I said earlier, there is something eerie about this mist. This is real Scotch Mist – you know, when the bogie men come out of it.' The taxi driver chuckled to himself. The green lights from the dashboard cast an eerie glow over his face, making his eyes very deep and mysterious, and his nose cast a large shadow over his thin, lined mouth. He was the only thing that looked eerie, thought Erin. She tutted and rolled her eyes, unimpressed.

'Mist, Scotch Mist, whatever mist – it's all the same to me.'

'Well ...' The taxi driver checked his rear view mirror before responding to Erin. Mrs Scott didn't seem to be angry with him this time – her head was lying back on the headrest and her eyes were closed. He was safe to continue.

'Well ... Scotch Mist is created by ...'

'I'm awake, you know,' snapped Brenda with her eyes still closed, 'so enough of your scare stories and get us home, please!'

Erin smiled at her mother. Not another word was said as the car silently penetrated the thick mist. She was almost hypnotised by the car lights dazzling back at her from the blanket of white mist.

Brodie was a bit squashed, but the car heating blasted under the seat and warmed him up nicely. His fur began to smell terribly as it dried out. Brenda sniffed the air and cast her eyes down at Erin's feet.

'What's in that bag?'

'Oh, it's just the bag. I ...er ... dropped it in the loch when I was down there. It's just drying quickly from the heat blasting under the seat. When I was taking photos, the rucksack slipped down my arm and fell in the water.' Erin cringed at more lies.

'Oh yes – that reminds me,' said Ralph thoughtfully. 'Pass your camera and I'll have a look at those photos I took last night of the animal pooh and the weird footprints. Got to convince dear old Rose Stewart that we have a case here, strange as it may seem. We definitely did not kidnap their dog. The whole thing is just too weird to be true. Finding Rusty's collar in our garden with that lucky white heather and that ... animal pooh. Weird. Very weird indeed.' He scratched his head and gazed into the mist.

Erin's heart palpitated hard against her rib cage. She had deleted the photos and she had since taken pictures of Brodie and Nessie with the camera, which she couldn't let her father see. Sweat prickled at her brow. 'Er ... Dad ... well ... uhm ...' Erin was trying to stall while thinking of a good enough excuse of what had happened to them. Of course!

'Dad, I'm really sorry, but when the bag fell from my arm, I dropped the camera in the loch too. I'm afraid the camera got a good soaking and I can't read any photos on it.' Guilt stabbed painfully at Erin's insides as she lied to her father. She hated lying to him – but she had to protect Brodie.

Ralph sighed heavily. 'Oh well, at least we have that bag of strange animal pooh. Once I've got that analysed, that might help to solve the mystery.'

Erin took a long, hard swallow as she remembered stuffing the bag into the rubbish bin. 'Er, Dad … I … er … threw it out.'

Her father shot a sudden look of panic her way. 'Why on earth did you do that, love?'

'Well, it was stinking the house out – I just thought I'd put it in the bin and then take it out before the rubbish was collected. But, I slept in this morning … remember?' she said trying to clutch at her father's softer side.

Ralph's world looked as though it had just fallen apart. How was he going to defend himself now against the Stewarts? They were impossible people. He sighed heavily again as the taxi continued to slice its way through the thickening mist.

The car screeched to an abrupt halt and everyone jolted forward, immediately restrained by their seatbelts. Brenda automatically grabbed Erin's arm. Brodie was thrust against the back of the seat in front of Erin, but as there was little room to go anywhere else he only suffered minor bruising on his back. Everyone sat dazed for a few moments, wondering why the car had stopped so suddenly. All they could see was mist.

Erin, Ralph and Brenda gasped and jerked their heads back into the seats as something ran out of the mist towards them. Four large steaming stags leapt over the car, one after the other, and landed effortlessly on the road behind them. The whites of their eyes dazzled against the car headlights, and steam bellowed from their nostrils into the frosty night air. They left as quickly as they had arrived.

'Wow – the Monarch of the Glen. What beautiful specimens – and what a rare sight these days.' Ralph watched the last of the four stags run into the mist, thrilled at what he had just seen. He released his grip on the seat and turned towards the taxi driver. 'That was a close call – well done. You've got marvellous eyesight. What's your name, by the way?' Ralph extended his hand in a friendly gesture.

'Fergus Munro,' the man replied politely and shook Ralph's hand before driving on carefully through the mist. 'Yes, I have good eyesight. Like I said earlier – you never know what's lurking there in the Scotch Mist.' He turned back to Erin and grinned widely.

Erin scoffed as she checked the rucksack. Brodie looked up at her and scowled. His neck hurt a little and his insides felt very queasy. Erin winked and smiled at him before replacing the flap over the bag.

After a long and slow journey, the car finally pulled into the driveway. Ralph hadn't taken his eyes from the road, worried in case something else came out at them. Brenda had kept a firm grip on Erin's arm and Erin had held on tight to the handles of the rucksack for fear of another sharp stop.

When the car stopped in front of their house, Erin bundled the rucksack into her arms, opened the car door and stumbled out onto the snowy drive. Brodie's head took the brunt of the fall as the rucksack dropped to the ground.

Fergus rushed around to Erin's aid and his face broke into a warm smile as he looked at Erin lying in the snow – unhurt. 'I remember my daughter when she was your age – always tripping up on her own feet. My wife enrolled her in ballet classes to help her balance. May I suggest ballet,' he chuckled, bending to help Erin to her feet.

Erin glared at the man and refused his help. She wasn't laughing so why should he be?

'You ok dear?' asked Ralph and Brenda rushing to her side.

'Well if she is, I'm not,' Brodie muttered to himself as he nursed his wounds. 'How much more of these humans can I suffer? Puleese will someone get me home?'

'Yes, I'm ok,' said Erin shooting a glance back at the car. 'I caught my foot on that thing.' She pointed back to something hanging out of the door. The taxi driver blocked their view as he leant inside the car and rummaged around.

'No – nothing in there my dear. Like I said, you must've tripped on your own feet. Or it could've been the Scotch Mist – it's a real curse.' He smiled gently as he picked up the rucksack and handed it back to her. He lowered his voice. 'Hope you haven't damaged anything in there.'

Erin froze for a few seconds. She snatched the bag from him and was about to protest about what she had tripped on when the man stared mysteriously at her. She couldn't explain the look in his eyes, but felt strangely compelled to remain silent. She simply nodded at him and walked up the garden path towards the house, which was almost entirely hidden by the mist. She looked back at Fergus Munro as he climbed into his car. Why hadn't she been able to defend herself back there? She stood and watched the car reverse out of the drive before turning and going inside.

Erin scaled the stairs two at a time and ran into her bedroom. Brodie's ears felt the familiar pop as she slammed the bedroom door before setting the rucksack on her bed and opening it.

Brodie was relieved to see Erin's shining blue eyes. He climbed out onto the bed and crouched on the soft quilt, sighing deeply. He didn't have the normal crystal-blue gaze of a lively ten-year old haggis – just a very serious look and frown. 'Here we go again,' he muttered sadly.

Slipping her father's coat from her shoulders, she hung it

over the door handle. She was exhausted. After hanging her clothes up in the wardrobe, she slipped into her aqua-green pyjamas and climbed wearily into bed.

'We need to think about what we're going to do. But not tonight. I'm tired.'

Brodie didn't argue. He crawled under the duvet and within seconds, the pains of the day drifted from his tired limbs as he slipped into a very comfortable sleep. Both of them were too tired to notice the growing tensions outside.

CHAPTER FIVE

Friend or Foe?

Brodie's eyes flicked open. Something had startled him from his deep sleep – but he wasn't sure what. He could hear Erin's delicate breathing as the bedcovers raised slightly then fell on each breath.

There was a muffled thud, followed by muffled cries. He strained to listen. They weren't cries. They sounded more like muffled arguing and fighting. There was another thud.

Brodie became restless. He couldn't just lie still – or wake Erin and let her deal with it. No – not Brodie. He went himself, while Erin continued her peaceful sleep. Edging down the bed until he was at the bottom of it, he carefully and silently pulled the duvet back so that his head was peering out into the darkened bedroom, barely lit by the green glow from Erin's alarm clock. He blinked widely at the sight before him.

Ralph's black coat was being tossed around the carpeted floor. First one way, then the other. It jumped once or twice, stopped for a few moments while it breathed heavily and then jumped around again, all the time arguing with itself.

Brodie chuckled until he realised that the coat shouldn't be alive. It was moving by itself. His eyes took on an air of curiosity as he continued to watch the coat wriggle around the floor. It jumped again, then rested for a short time. A muffled voice became angry and lumps appeared in the side of the coat as though something was throwing punches. Completely absorbed in the antics of the coat like a cat watching a mouse, Brodie laughed aloud.

The coat stopped moving and the muffled noises stopped.

A crack of light appeared under the bedroom door and lit up the coat as it lay crumpled on the floor. The door handle creaked downwards and a pale triangle of light formed across Erin's bed as the door opened slowly.

Brodie dropped the duvet over his head and remained very still.

'Erin? You ok?' Brenda peered in at Erin. She smiled warmly at the wild splash of red curly hair peeking above the duvet.

Erin continued to sleep and never responded to her mother. The last two days with Brodie had left her totally exhausted.

Brenda stood and listened to Erin's gentle breathing before closing the door again, satisfied that she was fast asleep. She was becoming concerned at her daughter's change in behaviour lately. She had run straight from the car and up to her room without kissing them goodnight. Without asking for her usual cup of hot chocolate before going to bed. It had been late for someone so young. Guilt stabbed at Brenda as she realised how absorbed she had been in the last few weeks organising the Burns Supper. She would arrange to take Erin out on a girls' only shopping day tomorrow.

As soon as the door clicked shut, Brodie leapt out from under the duvet and slowly, cautiously circled the black coat as it lay motionless. He sniffed at it like a dog.

'Erin? Erin? Is that you? Are you here? Where am I? Please … Erin … help me?' A pitiful, muffled voice trickled from the coat.

Brodie cocked his ginger-red head from side to side and his ears twitched with curiosity as he moved closer to the talking coat.

'Awe, Erin. Don't leave me here. I've changed – honest, I've changed … believe me, I have.' After a lot of huffing and puffing and grunting, the coat flew about a foot in the air, long enough for the ghillie dhu to run out from under it. He caught his foot in the torn pocket and fell flat on his face on the carpet.

Brodie laughed again. Then he stopped once he realised it was Booger – the evil ghillie dhu from the forest. But of course! Erin had taken the moss-speckled heather back from Dion Cameron. The spell had since worn off and the ghillie dhu was free once again.

Brodie looked at him with hesitation – was he friend or foe?

The little pixie-like man wrestled his legs free of the torn pocket and stood facing Brodie, looking him up and down carefully. After a few thoughtful moments, a large friendly smile split his wrinkled green face. 'Wow – what a great nose you have – I really like you Brodie! No, I really, really do,' he cooed childishly as he jumped up and down, clapping his hands excitedly.

Brodie frowned. Not twenty-four hours ago, this moss-covered excuse for a pixie was trying to kill both him and Erin. How could he change so suddenly? Was he trying to trick him?

The ghillie dhu moved closer to Brodie and stared right into his eyes. 'I like your eyes too – they're so blue. Not like mine. Mine are green and horrible. Yours are just sooooo lovely.' He stood in front of Brodie, swooning like he had been reacquainted with his first love. Pink hearts rose into the air from his chest and popped gently above his head.

'Booger – behave yourself. You don't like me more than a dog likes a cat, so stop pretending you do!'

The small ghillie dhu's ears drooped at Brodie's words and his harsh green eyes became saddened. He stood with a wounded posture. 'But Brodie – of course I like you. I LOVE you. I know I didn't – but things are different now. I want to be your friend – please ...?' Clasping his moss-covered hands together, he pressed them under his chin, went down on bended knee and pleaded with Brodie. 'And, you can call me Booger too – I like you calling me that.' His moss and fir-clad clothes trembled as he grinned cheesily at Brodie.

Brodie edged back from the ghillie dhu and snarled at him. It had to be a trick – it had to be. He couldn't be trusted in the forest – why should he trust him now? He tripled around the ghillie dhu, ready to head-butt him, but Booger simply stood like a servant in front of him, ready to take whatever Brodie was going to throw at him.

Erin stirred.

Brodie jumped up onto the bed and stumbled across the thick duvet to Erin's head. He tried pulling back the duvet, but couldn't because he was standing on it, so he leant over and flicked her forehead with his toe-like fingers.

'Come on Erin – wake up. We're in trouble and all you can do is sleep?' He flicked her head harder.

Erin brushed Brodie away sleepily, almost knocking him to the floor. He flicked her head again.

'Ow!'

'That's better – now listen to me will you?'

Erin held her hand over her head and stared sleepily at Brodie as he warned her that the ghillie dhu was back – in her bedroom. Erin shrugged her shoulders, shut her eyes and fell back onto her pillow. She smiled like a baby on a cloud of cotton wool and drifted back off to sleep.

'He's right – I'm back Erin, wake up. Wake up!' Booger jumped up on the bed beside her.

'Yeah, right and I've just turned into a princess. Now, where's my prince charming,' she sighed dreamily as pictures of Daniel Radcliffe entered her head.

Brodie and the ghillie dhu stood on either side of Erin and stared on silently.

Erin lay motionless for a few seconds as her thoughts became stronger. Her eyes flickered open and she saw clothing made out of fir leaves and moss. She closed her eyes and began drifting off to sleep again when realisation slapped her in the face.

Erin bolted upright and the ghillie dhu and Brodie catapulted to the floor like two rag dolls. Reaching over, she switched on her bedside lamp and scratched at her head with both hands. Brodie lay in a heap at one side of her bed and the ghillie dhu lay at the other side.

How could she have been so foolish? She had forgotten to

throw the heather away before leaving Urquhart Castle and now she had stupidly invited the ghillie dhu into her own home.

Brodie untangled his legs, rolled over and jumped back up onto the bed. Erin cradled him in her arms as they both looked down at the green ghillie dhu.

'He claims that he's changed – so friendly – you wouldn't believe. Yeuch – it's sickening.' Brodie shuddered.

'What about what you tried to do to us in the forest? Nobody likes you – not even the goblins do!' Erin protested hotly, her cheeks reddening to the colour of her hair.

The ghillie dhu simply smiled back at them like an excited puppy, begging for their forgiveness.

'Erin – maybe he has changed ... remember what you said about my power and anything I changed into heather would become my friend when the spell wore off? Remember Rusty?'

Erin looked long and hard at the quivering heap of leaves and she looked back at Brodie. He was gullible, but surely not that gullible. Gertruda hadn't changed into a friend – so what made them believe that Booger had really changed?

The floorboards in her parents' room creaked.

'Quick – both of you – get under the bed!' she instructed in a strained whisper. Brodie immediately ran under the bed, making sure not to bump into the leg this time. Booger remained where he was, unsure of the urgency. 'Quick Booger – get your mossy backside under this bed – NOW!'

'What's going on in here?' asked Brenda. Strands of dishevelled hair fell down around her face and her normally straight blonde fringe was matted and stuck to the sides of her forehead. Dark shadows circled her eyes as the strains of the previous day showed on her face. She was a long way from the perfection she looked at the Burns Supper. She yawned heavily and placed her hand over her mouth.

'Oh, I think I was dreaming, Mum. Er ... something about

Scotch Mist and monsters.'

Brenda padded across the carpet in her bare feet and pressed the back of her hand against Erin's forehead. 'No obvious signs of a temperature. It's been those ridiculous stories from that stupid taxi driver. I'll complain to his company in the morning – frightening young girls like that. Who does he think he is? See, you may say that you don't believe any of that stuff, but the subconscious mind is stronger than you think.'

Erin lay back down in her bed and pulled the duvet up to her chin as she listened to her mother mutter about the inconsiderate taxi driver. Erin had never had a nightmare in her life, but it's the first thing that she could think of to say to her mother.

As Brenda turned to leave the bedroom, she noticed Ralph's coat lying in a crumpled heap on the floor and tutted loudly.

'Sorry Mum, it must've fallen off the door handle when you came in.' She hoped her mother wouldn't notice the torn lining. She had to get the coat back from her mother to fix it.

'You should've left this downstairs for me to put away,' she tutted again, draping the coat across her arm and smoothing out the creases. 'It's expensive and doesn't belong on the floor.' She yawned widely and padded back out of the room. 'Ouch!' Brenda hopped in pain after standing on something sharp. She bent down to the floor and picked up the piece of red porcelain. 'What on earth's this?' she asked, hopping in pain.

Erin hesitated. 'Oh, can you just leave it by my computer. I found it and want to look at its history – see if there's any writing on it and what not. See how old it is.'

Brenda frowned as she placed it beside the computer. 'I could've cut my foot on that …'

'And if you just leave the coat on the chair I'll brush all of the hairs from it tomorrow and hang it back up. You know what Dad's like – if he sees one hair on it, he'll be wiping the coat down for weeks until there's no coat left!'

Brenda turned and smiled at her daughter, setting the coat on the chair. 'Yes, you're right, love. You de-hair it and get it back into the cupboard before your father gets a chance to go near it. Otherwise he'll drive us both nuts!' She crossed her eyes and made a face as they laughed girlishly.

'Sleep tight …'

'… and don't let the bed bugs bite,' said Erin finishing the sentence as she always did.

Brenda bent down and pressed her lips to Erin's pale forehead kissing her good night. She smiled warmly at her daughter as she backed out of the room.

'Which reminds me Mum – I left my coat back at the castle. We were in such a rush for the taxi that I forgot to pick it up on the way out.'

Brenda frowned sleepily. 'I'll get it in the morning – now sleep well.'

'I'll just leave my light on, and I'll play some music. I think that way I'll sleep easier. Just in case you hear more noise – it's only music.'

'As long as it's not too loud – I need my beauty sleep.' Brenda leaned over the dressing table and checked her eyes in the mirror. She sighed and pinched at the skin under them. 'Goodness knows where all those bags came from. Looks like a family of four has just moved in for a ten-month holiday with the size of bags they have brought with them. Wonder if I've any chance of evicting them by the morning?'

Erin laughed. 'Mum – you're just being silly. You're beautiful and I don't see any bags.'

Brenda kissed the palm of her hand and blew across it in Erin's direction. Erin raised her hand and grabbed at the air.

'Caught it – and here's one back.' She kissed her hand and blew across it in her mother's direction.

Brenda grabbed at the air and caught the kiss. 'I'll just put it in my pocket and keep it for when I get tucked up in bed. Love you.'

'Love you too.'

Brenda let out a large tired sigh as she closed the door and padded back up the corridor to her bedroom. Erin was growing up far too fast. A tear trickled from the edge of her eye and down her smooth skin. She climbed back into bed and switched off her light, listening for Erin. She heard some light music, which got a little louder and she listened to Ralph's breathing. Then darkness swept over her and she drifted back into a much-needed sleep.

Sounds of heartfelt sobbing drifted out from under Erin's bed.

'What's going on down there?' she demanded, turning the volume of the music up slightly to drown out the sobs.

'Oooh – that's just sooo lovely. So sad. You have a wonderful, wonderful mother ... and that music is just … just magic, boo hoo …'

Brodie looked at the sobbing ghillie dhu as he continued to wail. Snot dribbled from his pointed nose and saliva dribbled from his quivering mouth.

'Pull yourself together Booger,' Brodie snorted. 'What happened to the strong, evil little pixie-man that we fought against back in the forest?' Brodie remained suspicious of his intentions.

Booger sobbed even louder. 'I told you … I'm so sorry about all that, I've been a horrible, horrible, horrible ghillie dhu and I never ever want to go back to the forest ever, ever again. I will have so many enemies in there – I just couldn't cope with all that hate. Can't I have at least one friend – can't that be you, Brodie?' He howled out the words and wiped his fir-covered arm across his face, sniffing in heavily.

Brodie retched silently as the glistening saliva and snot clung to Booger's arm. He could see why Gertruda had named him so. 'Well – the name Booger suits you, so you'll have to get used to your name if you want to be friends.'

The ghillie dhu replaced his sorrowful frown with a large appreciative smile. 'Who cares what you call me – I have a friend!' He started to plant kisses all over Brodie's face.

'And will you STOP DOING THAT! No kissing – just remember that!' Brodie ran to the corner of the room.

Booger composed himself and sat down in front of Brodie, a wide smile dividing his, now happy, face. 'Whatever you say, friend. I've got a friend. I've never had a friend before. It feels good good GOOD! Brodie – I really like you – you've got a lovely nose,' he said raising his hand to touch it. 'A really, really lovely nose.'

Brodie leapt out of his way and arched his back like a cat.

Booger hissed at him and showed his fangs, but quickly retreated. 'Er, sorry – it will take some time getting used to being good,' he apologised, shamefully. 'But, I will. Really I will. I really, really will …'

Erin bowed her head to her hands and groaned miserably. Now she had twice the trouble to deal with. As if a haggis wasn't enough!

CHAPTER SIX

The Curse of The Scotch Mist

No wonder the ghillie dhu had been such a miserable creature – anyone would be if they had to spend their life in the dark and dingy forest with so many enemies, Erin thought as she spread out a fleece jacket for him to wrap himself up in. He was certainly wrapped. Erin had never seen someone smile so gratefully.

'Thank you Erin. Thank you. It's so kind of you. I am so grateful. Really I am. Truly. It's so great to have you as a friend too. I just want to talk to you forever. Don't leave me when I sleep – promise?'

Erin shook her head as the ghillie dhu continued to babble on, and on, and on.

'Now, Brodie snores and I have to poke him in the side to keep him quiet – otherwise he'd be under here with you as well.'

'I can poke him in his side too if he snores. I'd just sit and watch him all night and I could keep him quiet. Please, please, please Erin?' He clapped his hands together like a child and his eyes sparkled with youth. 'In fact – I don't mind him snoring. As long as he's my friend – he can snore all he wants to. As loud as he wants. Forever, and ever, and ever …'

Erin smiled as she pushed the ghillie dhu under the bed and assured him that she could cope. Brodie had to get some sleep after all. She stared at the funny little man and shook her head dismissively. It was only yesterday that he had whinged about the haggises' snoring sending his great grandfather mad and how he too had vowed revenge on the haggis. Could he really have changed?

'You know, Brodie,' she said climbing back under her duvet. 'Maybe he has changed. If it wasn't for the scar above Rusty's left eye, Rose would never have believed it was the same dog either.'

Erin's eyes drifted into space as she saw William Stewart's handsome face, but the image was quickly wiped away as she recalled watching her neighbour throw a stick at the poor suffering dog, wounding him above the eye. He had a wicked temper and was always tormenting their poor dog – and her. He seemed to enjoy making enemies. A bit like Booger … used to be.

Brodie stared at Erin thoughtfully. 'What's wrong?'

'How on earth are we going to stop Gertruda?'

Erin and Brodie stared at one another for some time until Erin eventually fell asleep. Brodie snuggled up to Erin and eventually fell asleep too. The ghillie dhu snuggled up in Erin's fleece under the bed and smiled contentedly when he heard Brodie begin to snore.

Erin was even more tired today as she lay under the duvet and contemplated how Brodie was going to end Gertruda's vengeance. She suddenly became aware of a pair of green eyes staring intensely at her.

'Good morning, Erin.'

She blinked widely at the ghillie dhu sitting in the chair at the side of her bed. He smiled at Erin, beckoning her to return his gesture. He looked like a small rag doll in an oversized chair.

Erin managed to break a smile. 'Good morning … Booger. How long have you been sitting there? What if someone had come in?'

'Oh, not long – just a few hours. No one will see me – only you can – so I didn't really need to hide when your mother came in last night. It's so nice to watch you breath,' he said sincerely. 'I really like having two friends. It's a great feeling. A really great feeling. A really, really great feeling.' The ghillie dhu displayed his teeth through a very appreciative smile. 'What can I do for you today? Can we play?'

Erin studied the strange little man. He looked somewhat

youthful, but the many lines on his face showed that he was very old – maybe more than a hundred. A little old man wanting to play like a child – it was weird. Really, really weird. Really, really, really weird. She shook her head and slapped her forehead. She was beginning to sound like him already.

Brodie sighed heavily as he heard Booger's steely voice. He stuck his head out from under the duvet. 'No playing today. Today we have to find Gertruda.'

The ghillie dhu's eyes filled up with fear. 'I don't want to find Gertruda. You'll never beat her. Please, don't make me go back there,' he begged.

'But we have to. I have to save the haggis.' Brodie's face filled with strain and his young eyes took on the wisdom of an old man. 'Are you going to help us?'

The ghillie dhu jumped down from the green chair and began pacing the floor, his hands behind his back as he walked a few steps, turned and walked back a few steps.

'On one condition,' he finally answered.

'What?' snapped Brodie.

'That you'll be my friend forever and ever and ever?'

Brodie didn't think that he would last a day being in the annoying ghillie dhu's company never mind being a life-long friend.

Erin noticed Brodie's hesitation. 'Yes, of course he will. Now – what are we going to do?'

The ghillie dhu looked perplexed and fidgeted with his hands. 'Why are you asking me?'

'Because you know Gertruda. You know how to get to her. You know what her weaknesses are.'

Booger shook his head and began to tremble.

'Is that a no?' Brodie was losing his patience.

Booger continued to tremble.

'Well? Friend for life or not?'

Booger's face instantly lit up at the thought of a friend for life. Then the enthusiasm faded. He paused for a few moments before agreeing to help them.

Erin climbed out of bed, slipped her feet into her slippers and padded across the bedroom to the window. She threw open the curtains and was almost knocked off her feet as bright, white light gushed in and blinded her. She squinted until her eyes became used to the intense light. The mist was like a wall of pure white snow – she couldn't see beyond the window.

Brodie jumped up onto the windowsill, pleased of some daylight, but he was knocked back by the powerful glare. 'Wow, that is some mist.' He shielded his eyes.

'Mist?' said the ghillie dhu. 'Mist? I haven't seen mist for … gee, I forget. It's been so long since I've been out of the forest. Let's see.' He climbed up the curtain, stood on the windowsill beside his new best friend and stared on in silence.

'Oh dear,' he said eventually. 'Oh deary, deary me.'

Brodie turned towards him. 'What?'

'Oh deary, deary, deary me. It's … Scotch Mist.'

Erin flicked her eyes to the ghillie dhu and then back to the mist. She ran her fingers through her red curls and combed out some of the knots. 'Mist? Scotch Mist? It's all the same to me. What's the problem?' She yawned widely and rubbed at her left eye with the back of her hand.

'Don't you know? Don't you see?'

Brodie became uneasy at Booger's sudden change in behaviour and voice. He became almost delirious and began hopping around the room. 'Oh no. Oh no. Oh no. Not this again. Oh noooo!'

'It's not what? Will you stop jumping around you silly old fool.' Erin placed her hand on the ghillie dhu's small shoulder. 'Now calm down and tell us what on earth has sparked you off?'

The ghillie dhu lifted his head and looked into Erin's blue eyes. Erin looked back at him, waiting for an answer. His eyes had become luminous. She took a sharp intake of breath and grabbed Brodie. 'Quick – his eyes. Don't look at his eyes. I knew he hadn't changed – he's trying to hex us.'

The ghillie dhu's eyes turned red and saliva foamed at the corners of his mouth.

'Quick Brodie – he needs to be heather again before he does damage to us. Stay away from his arms – once they're around us we'll be enslaved to him, and probably Gertruda, forever!'

Booger finally snapped out of his stupor and blinked widely as his eyes returned to their lesser, luminous green colour. He looked at them apologetically. 'I told you, we're friends for life. I'm not about to do anything to hurt you – please believe me.' He turned back towards the window and shuddered. 'We are all in danger now.'

'What do you mean?' asked Brodie impatiently. He jumped back up onto the windowsill, screeched loudly and somersaulted backwards, crashing heavily onto the floor.

Erin's heart leapt out of her mouth. 'Get under the bed now – both of you. Mum will be in here thinking that I've fallen out of bed – quick!'

Erin ran over to the television set, switched it on and scattered some books on the floor. Then she sat on her bed nursing her big toe. She was right. Within seconds, her bedroom door flew open.

'Erin? Are you alright dear?'

Erin spoke to her mother through a fake, injured voice. 'I just tripped over those books and stubbed my toe,' she whined.

Brenda looked at the pile of books on the floor. 'What have I told you about leaving things lying around? Are you in much pain? Is anything broken?' she asked leaning over Erin's foot and gently massaging her toe.

'It'll be alright, Mum. It was more of a shock, I think. Yes, I'll put the books away.'

Brenda looked around the room. 'I thought I heard bagpipes – what are you watching on the TV?'

Erin looked up. 'Don't know – but there was something similar sounding on it – not really sure. I'll be fine.'

After Brenda had made sure that Erin's toe wasn't broken, she asked her to get dressed. 'Your famous friend, Dion Cameron telephoned to invite us to lunch at Skibo Castle today. Wear something nice. Just wait until I tell them at work about this – my daughter – invited to lunch by Dion Cameron – I still can't believe it!' Brenda's mascara-lined eyes filled with excitement.

Erin's insides churned. What if she asked to see the haggis again? Her mother would want to know more. She had no time to dine with the rich and famous. She had to get back to the forest. She couldn't leave Brodie on his own either – especially with Booger around. She stood up and faked a limp.

'Ouch. I don't think that I'm going to be able to put any shoes on. I can't even walk on it. I'll have to stay at home.'

Brenda looked down at her daughter's small foot. 'Oh Erin – you can't miss this. Think of what you could tell all of your friends at school! We'll carry you if we need to.'

'That would be really embarrassing, Mum. I can't go!'

Brenda looked at her daughter with surprise. Her weird behaviour was beginning to worry her. She would never normally act in such a way. There had to be something more wrong with her. She knew how she'd get her to go.

'Oh well – if you insist. I'll just phone Rose and ask her to take you for the day. I'm sure you and William can play on the computer or build snowmen or something …'

Erin protested strongly. 'You can't do that to me. And what about the mist – look – how can you drive in that?'

'You know, it's the strangest mist I've even seen. It is across the loch and surrounds our house, but Rose has just phoned and she doesn't have any mist at all. She can't see our house because it's just buried in it – wonder why? Suppose it has to start and stop somewhere.'

Erin looked towards the window. What had Brodie seen out there that had caused him to fall off the windowsill in such a way?' She muttered a few words about her sore toe and agreed to go to Skibo Castle. She wasn't about to be left with the Stewarts, but she would have to take Brodie and Booger with her.

Brenda smiled triumphantly as she walked out of the room. 'Rose Stewart is complaining again that someone's nicked her ghastly gnome. Your father has finally managed to persuade her that we didn't kidnap her precious dog. But it's very strange, all the same.' When the bedroom door clicked shut Erin crouched on the floor and peered under the bed.

'Boo!'

Brodie and Booger jumped with fright and hit their heads on the bottom of the bed. Erin laughed softly.

'Will you stop doing that to me Erin,' Brodie snapped as he rubbed his head. 'What's happened to Gnogard now? Did those things in the mist get him?'

Erin's eyebrows knitted together in a frown. 'We left Gnogard at Urquhart Castle – remember? You turned him into heather. Anyway, what things in the mist?'

Booger slid out from under the bed and began to pace the room again, twisting his hands together in nervous frustration as he paced. 'The Scotch Mist, like I said. It's trouble. Trouble, trouble, trouble! Oh dear. Oh my. We're in B-I-G trouble.' He continued to pace frantically, muttering to himself.

Brodie jumped in front of the ghillie dhu and head-butted him to the floor. 'Stop your havering and tell us what you mean!'

The ghillie dhu stopped talking, but continued to tremble. He stood up and pointed to the window.

'You saw it for yourself. Do you really need m-m-me to s-s-spell it out for y-y-you?' Without moving his head, Booger shifted his eyes nervously to the window and then back to Erin before responding. 'Go have a look … tell me what you see …'

Brodie and Erin quickly exchanged glances. Brodie had seen something in the mist, but he wasn't sure what. Erin scooped him up in her arms and went to the window.

Brodie craned his neck to see and gasped loudly.

Erin nearly let him fall as she gasped too.

'See them? See what I mean? That's Scotch Mist …'

Brodie jolted back in Erin's arms as he watched the creatures lunge at the window. Erin tightened her arms around him and watched the strange creatures darting around in the mist. There were hundreds of them. Mist-like. Some large; some small and some very, very frightening.

Brodie shrieked at the mist ball that fired towards them. It stopped abruptly at the window, uncurled itself and revealed an angry face with three eyes staring at them. The middle eye pulsed red. Two long fangs extended from its upper jaws. The large creature was butted out of the way by a small, yellow creature who hovered at the window and giggled at them. He looked comical as his eyes rolled around in his head at different speeds and in different directions. He shivered like a bowl of jelly as he giggled, and his tongue flapped around loosely. Brodie laughed. So did Erin, but their smiles faded quickly as another mist-spirit lunged at the window. She had blood-red lips, wriggling worms on her eyebrows and scars over her ghostly-white face. She looked down her turned up nose and flashed her cold, purple eyes at them.

Brodie could not only see the creatures now, he could hear them.

'Nah, nah na-na naaaahh,' they kept saying over, and over again. They laughed, joked and screamed continuously as they lunged at the window – some had wide eyes; some had only one; some laughed their heads off, then picked them up and put them back on their shoulders; one of the creatures cheekily wiggled his large stomach at them and burped loudly. He laughed insanely and waved frantically at them with his ghostly hands. What were they all finding so funny?

Brodie sprung from Erin's arms and stormed across to Booger. 'What's the Scotch Mist all about? What are those things out there and why does it mean trouble?'

Booger bowed his head. 'I'm afraid it's the Curse of the Scotch Mist and it looks like it's one of us who is cursed.

Erin knelt down beside Brodie and the ghillie dhu. 'Tell us more.'

'Well,' he continued. 'Those things out there – the mist-spirits – only show themselves when there's trouble in their world. They live just below the surface in such a tranquil and pleasant place. However, when they are troubled, mist rises from the ground. The Scotch Mist is the only mist that rises from the ground and it is so thick that you can never normally see beyond your nose.'

'Seems like most of those creatures out there are thick,' said Erin sarcastically.

Booger raised his hand to his nose and scratched at it as he continued. 'The Scotch Mist is normally only found in isolated patches – around the person or thing that is being cursed.

Erin stared at Booger thoughtfully. 'So the taxi driver was right then.'

The ghillie dhu felt slightly uncomfortable. 'Taxi driver?'

Erin waved her hand to dismiss her thoughts and encouraged the ghillie dhu to continue.

Brodie was becoming impatient. 'So what is causing this? What is the curse?'

'What happens if we go out in it?' asked Erin. 'I mean – are my parents safe walking in the mist? Am I safe?'

'Unless they believe in our world, they'll never know that the spirits are even there, and I doubt that they'll ever see into this world at their age. Only very few children see us and they are believed to be talking to their imaginary friends. Over time, as their parents continue to disbelieve them, they soon find other things to do and stop being able to see us. I don't know why you've managed to come through to our world,' he said looking back at Erin. 'You're older than the normal child who makes contact with us.'

Erin shrugged her shoulders and urged him to continue.

'But, those humans who are in our world, are at risk.' He looked sadly into Erin's widened eyes. 'I can only assume it's got something to do with Gertruda and she won't let up until she's got what she wants …' He drifted his gaze to Brodie.

Brodie jumped up and down in front of Booger. 'What do the mist-spirits want?'

'Well … your guess is as good as mine … but I would guess that the mist-spirits are afraid that Gertruda is close to achieving her life-long vow. The only way she can die peacefully is to follow that vow through – to kill every haggis around. And when she dies, she will join the mist-spirits. They want to keep her alive as long as possible because they're so frightened she'll destroy their sanctuary. She'll take over – just like her mother did until they got rid of her, but it was a painful experience for them until they did.'

Booger ran his finger up the inside of his nose.

'Eeeewwweee!' Erin screwed up her face and almost vomited as he removed a large piece of slime, but Booger didn't seem to understand Erin's disgust at his action as he licked his finger enjoyably.

'You have a very appropriate name,' Erin said clutching at her throat in disgust. 'So, what is the curse?'

Booger hesitated. He seemed to struggle getting the words out. 'They … w-will try and k-k-keep you away f-f-from Gertruda.'

'But we HAVE to face her again. She knows too much now. The Secret of Loch Ness is in danger. She could return to Drumdrui.'

'There's something else …'

'What, Booger? What else?' Erin was becoming frustrated with his long and drawn out tale.

'Another element. There is another strong faerie involved in this – there has to be. I don't think they're trying to send you home just yet Brodie – they're guarding the loch.'

'What will they do to me?'

The ghillie dhu looked at Brodie and was about to open his mouth to respond when he decided not to.

'Booger?'

He sighed and hesitated. 'They will follow you for the rest of your life, and probably you too Erin. You will always be shrouded in mist. They … they ….'

'For goodness sake Booger – spit it out!'

'They sing terribly. They will tell you the most terrible jokes and they will laugh loud in your face – day and night. Until you give in and give them what they want. You will be eternally cursed.'

'Is that all?' Erin laughed. 'You call that a curse?'

'You will become miserable – never seeing sunshine – never having peace. Erin – this is no laughing matter.'

'Will they come into the house?' Brodie asked as he watched the yellow mist-spirit bumble around in front of him with his eyes rolling uncontrollably.

'No, they won't come inside a house in case they get stuck. If they stay out of the mist for too long they will die.'

'But I thought they were already dead?!' Brodie was shocked.

'Yes, yes – they're dead in a respect – but because they're mist-spirits they still live in the undead world. If they die again then they're gone forever. And they will be frightened that that could happen if Gertruda joins them.'

Erin pulled the curtains together snapping out the glare from the mist, but the babble from the mist-spirits was very distinct. Her ears were already beginning to suffer from the Curse.

CHAPTER SEVEN

Escape to Skibo Castle

Mist-spirits of all shapes, sizes and colours lunged at the car as Erin's father steered it down the driveway and onto the main road. Some of them flew past the car. Some of them bounced off the windscreen, but her parents didn't notice a thing.

'I've never seen such thick mist before,' said Brenda as she leaned forward and squinted her eyes to try and see through it. 'Rose said that it will disappear just around the corner, but I'm doubting it at the moment.'

'Well, the taxi driver did say that it was Scotch Mist. Maybe something will jump out at us!' laughed Ralph.

Brenda scowled. Just at that moment, the large mist-spirit with the two long fangs and three eyes across his face appeared at the window beside Erin. His middle eye pulsed red. Erin screamed.

'See, look what you've done to your daughter now! Are you ok Erin?' Brenda leaned over her seat to look at Erin, who was staring at the ugly spirit as it attached misty suckers to the car window. She followed her daughter's frightened gaze out of the window and spoke to her soothingly.

'It's ok love, it's only mist and nothing will jump out at you. Your father thinks he's being funny, but trust me, he isn't.' She glared at Ralph, who decided it was better to drive on in silence.

The large mist-spirit clung onto the window as Erin continued to stare back at it. Brodie growled quietly from the rucksack. Erin had opened the flap to give him some air and daylight. She looked across to Booger who was on the seat next to her. Booger was right. If only believers could see into his world, then he could quite easily walk around without being noticed by her parents. He was on his knees with his face buried into the back of the seat to avoid looking at any of the spirits. All she could see was his trembling bottom.

Booger wailed loudly as he repeated how much danger they were in. 'How are we going to get out of here alive? Oooh – I've never been so scared – I want my forest back, boo hoo …'

Brodie stared angrily at the bumbling wreck – some help he would be in trying to get them all out of danger. 'Oh shut up you pile of useless moss – get a grip of yourself.' We're relying on you,' he hissed, but it was too late – it was out before he realised it. Erin tugged hard at the bag and Brodie banged his head on the back of the seat.

'Ouch!'

'What was that dear?' asked Brenda turning around in her seat again to look at Erin.

Erin smiled back sheepishly. 'Oh … just muttering to myself Mum.'

'Sounded a bit strange to me – are you sure you're alright – is your throat sore? I think we should get you to the doctors and get you checked out.'

Erin smiled sweetly and listened to her mother as she chattered to Ralph about Erin's behaviour and how he should stop trying to frighten her with his nonsense stories.

Just a few minutes' drive from the house the mist began to clear. The mist-spirit suckered to the window grew weaker as the car moved further and further from the mist until he eventually let go. Booger jumped up onto the back window and wagged his tongue at the spirit and as he limped back to the mist.

'Do you think that's really going to help?' Erin hissed.

Booger looked at Erin's angry face and jumped back down into his seat like a scolded child. 'They will catch up,' he whimpered. 'They will. And then we'll be in trouble, trouble, trouble.'

'What's that love?'

Erin looked at her mother's eyes in the vanity mirror.

'Nothing Mum – I was just talking to myself again.'

'You haven't got those imaginary friends again have you? You're a bit old for that now. You used to talk to imaginary friends when you were younger, remember?' Brenda smiled at her daughter as she remembered Erin's younger days.

'I don't remember having imaginary friends.' Erin squinted her eyes as she tried to remember, but nothing came to her. She didn't have imaginary friends now either – come to think of it, they were very real and most of them weren't even her friends. As she began to doubt her own mind again, she reached down and pulled her sock away from her ankle. The goblin bite she'd received at the Burns' Supper the evening before was still there. No – they weren't imaginary – they were very real. So, maybe the imaginary friends her mother was referring to were real as well.

After a pleasant drive through the snow-laden hillside, Ralph pulled the car up in front of Skibo Castle. It stood in all its splendour, ready to welcome more guests. Ready to make their visit the best they'd ever experienced – a well-kept Highland secret.

Erin held her breath whilst she absorbed the surroundings and the extensive gardens that were covered in creamy snow. She looked from window, to window, to window, as she imagined the large expensively decorated rooms that lay beyond them. She was beginning to feel like a princess. In a giddy pleasure, she climbed out of the car, making sure that Booger was beside her before she slammed the door shut.

'Erin – must you slam doors?' her father asked tirelessly. He had lost count of the number of times she'd been reminded.

Erin wasn't listening – she was still absorbing the splendour of the castle, imagining herself as a beautiful princess living in it.

Booger looked up at the castle in utter amazement. He was gobsmacked. 'So this is why so many escape to Skibo Castle for their holidays … and to get away from any trouble in the forest.'

'What?' quizzed Erin staring down at the green ghillie dhu as he continued to gaze up at the magnificent building.

'I've heard so much about this place, but never had the pleasure of seeing it,' he mused, scratching his head. 'I didn't believe that it really existed – I thought that everyone was just trying to be cruel to me, but … wow … this is just fantasticosa.' He wandered, unseen, between the adults as they were greeted by tall dark-haired men in kilts at the bottom of the grand steps that lead to an even grander entrance way. Some adults bumped into him which he tutted at, but nobody saw or felt him. Erin thought it amazing that he could go so unnoticed when she could see and hear him as clear as day.

'Hi there Hamish – staying long?'

Erin swung around to see who Booger was talking to.

Brodie peered out of the rucksack and watched silently.

'Hi there Snotbucket – just here for a few days' escape. What are you doing out of your forest? Finally decided to escape to Skibo Castle too? Told you it was great, didn't I?'

The ghillie dhu giggled boyishly as he walked back to Erin. 'Hi there you guys – escaping too?' he laughed as he waved at some smiling heather-pixies making their way to the front door of the castle. They shrieked and flapped their wings nervously as they tried to avoid him. The last time they'd seen him, he had told them to leave his forest and not to come back until he needed them again or they'd pay the price.

'It's only me,' he grinned cheesily. 'Your friendly ghillie dhu.'

'Don't tell us you're on holiday too, Booger. Didn't think you'd ever leave that forest of yours. Who's looking after it now? We hear that Gertruda wants your guts for garters.' The heather-pixies giggled childishly and flew on towards the castle steps and their luggage flew on after them – always staying the same distance behind their masters. The luggage was made of leaves, heather, gorse, and wood, all tightly woven into different types of stylish bags. They were stained a multitude of colours and some were eloquently embroidered. No bag was identical and each one bore its own name.

Booger began to tremble as more goblins and forest faeries arrived at the castle, each one with a bag or suitcase following on behind them, obediently. Something was going down and he wasn't sure he liked the feel of it.

Brodie tried not to blink in case he missed anything. The castle grounds were simply buzzing with hundreds of odd-looking creatures of different shapes, sizes and origin. Some of the creatures were checking out; some were running out of the castle to greet new arrivals, and some were being evicted by the foot-high, peaty-skinned boglouts.

Erin walked around in circles in disbelief. Goblins shimmying up drainpipes were quickly kicked back down by boglouts. 'Use the entrance and pay your fee,' they spat.

The weirdest looking birds that Brodie had ever seen were landing in the castle grounds, laden with dozens of faeries whose luggage flew on behind like a school of fish. The birds refuelled on some snow, because the pond was frozen over, loaded up with another batch of creatures leaving the castle and soared up to the sky, passing more birds arriving with even more creatures escaping to Skibo Castle. It was busier than Heathrow Airport, and much noisier.

'Hurry up – we've been waiting all morning for you. Would've liked the holiday to be in summer, but with what's going on down at the loch and in the forest just now, I wanted to be well clear of it. Don't know who's head is going to roll over this latest issue.' A very large heather-pixie flew down the stone steps to greet his friends as they arrived. He laughed menacingly as he crunched on a large piece of carrot that he'd just stolen from the kitchen. 'As always – the food is excellent here. Now, come along – check yourselves in and then meet me inside – lunch is about to be served!'

The heather-pixies ooh'd and aah'd at the thought of the magnificent food that the castle served up. They stopped at the boglouts' small reception desk at the foot of the stairs to check in. The boglouts' deep brown faces were stern as they surveyed everyone entering the castle and took one thistle penny from each of the heather-pixies for each night they wanted to stay. The booking fee allowed each guest to be checked into a room in the castle for the number of days requested, to roam the castle at will, to eat as much as they could and to fill their luggage with discarded items and food. The boglouts also kept guests alert of any dangers, including cats, dogs, birds and other enemies such as humans that believed in their world.

A rather plump goblin was being dragged out of the castle against his will by three sneering boglouts. He burped loudly through a face full of custard and cream.

'I've paid for three nights, so hands off!' he protested hotly.

'Yes – and those three nights were up two nights ago!' spat one of the boglouts. 'Now get your big bahooch out of this castle and don't come back until you've got some more thistle pennies.' The boglouts pushed him over the top step. He lost his footing and tumbled head over heels down the steps to the bottom. He lay sprawled out on the gravel and looked up at Erin and Booger, running his tongue around his face to clean the rest of the custard and cream from it.

'Worth a try,' he said wryly as he raised himself from the ground and winked at Booger. 'Yer cannae blame a loon for trying to get a good deal.' He burped loudly from both ends and staggered away from them, laughing dizzily. 'I tell you, the sherry trifle is fabulous. Just fabulous …' He hiccupped and burped and then laughed loudly.

'Why, that goblin's drunk,' retorted Erin, totally absorbed in the surroundings.

The goblin turned around and fired a look of surprise at her. 'You can't be talking to me, surely lass? You cannae see me, surely?'

'Course I can,' Erin replied tartly.

'Come on love – we're going in now. Who were you talking to?'

Erin looked up at her mother, startled.

Worry lines were beginning to show on Brenda's smooth face as she grew concerned about her daughter's growing habit of talking to herself. She blamed herself at having neglected her too much over the past few weeks – a girl's shopping treat was definitely on the cards. It would have to wait until tomorrow now.

Erin looked back at the goblin and winked at him. He responded with a glare before wobbling away from the castle.

Booger followed on behind Erin and laughed back at the goblin as the boglouts made sure he left the castle. 'She can see me too – so I get to stay in the castle for free because I'm with her!' He lifted his leafy shirt and wiggled his moss-covered backside at the boglouts.

'Reckon, do you?' Five boglouts, saliva dribbling from their sharp fangs, immediately surrounded Booger with their palms stretched out. 'Thistle pennies or you don't get past the door.'

'But … but, I'm with them – and I'm only here for lunch!' he said feeling a little less confident now.

'Pay up or stay out!'

'Do you know who I am?' The ghillie dhu squared up his small shoulders and tried to exert an air of importance.

'Hey boys, there's a ghillie dhu here who doesn't know who he is! Can anyone help him?!' The boglouts roared with snivelling laughter, which angered Booger. 'Why Snotbucket, it doesn't matter who you are, when you're outside of your forest – you play by our rules so pay up or stay out.' The leaves on the ghillie dhu's body began to quake and his eyes turned to a luminous green.

Erin bent down and pushed her face in between Booger and the boglouts. 'Look you little pooh sticks – he's with me and that's an order from my world. Now bog off and leave him alone – or Brodie will turn you into heather!'

The devilish boglouts stopped sniggering and their peaty faces dropped like lead. A deathly silence followed as every faerie in the castle grounds turned around and faced Erin.

'You mean HE's here?' gulped one of the boglouts.

Erin realised that they must have heard how Brodie had zapped a number of their friends and relations to heather, plus all of the ravens and some of the goblins, Booger and of course, Gertruda.

'Well, I've seen how nice and nancy pancy my cousins became after the spell wore off. I don't want to be like that!'

'Nor do we!' the rest of the faeries shouted.

'Well, you won't be,' retorted Erin. 'If you just let us be, then you'll be ok.'

The boglouts' black claws glinted as they repeatedly thumped their spiked tails on the ground in anger. They reluctantly parted and let the ghillie dhu through, watching on in silence as he and Erin climbed the steps into the castle. Brodie chuckled to himself. He felt a huge surge of power flow through his veins as he watched the speechless faces. From nobody back at home listening to his whines and questions about the myths and legends, to him being part of those myths and legends and becoming so powerful that they were all afraid of him. He couldn't help but gloat. Then the gloating turned to sadness as he reminded himself of the danger he had put the haggises in by being too inquisitive. He was no hero – he was just a common troublemaker.

'Some holiday this has turned into. How can we have fun with that haggis here? We need to do something about that,' said one of the boglouts cruelly. 'We need to let Gertruda know that he's here ...' The others nodded in agreement with him and thumped their spiked tails hard on the ground as they huddled together in a scrum, plotting their revenge.

CHAPTER EIGHT

Trouble at Drumdrui

Jock and Holly McHaggis emerged from the burrow tussled and tired, just barely aware that there had been some commotion outside. Since Brodie's disappearance over two days ago, they hadn't slept, until tonight.

Jock felt sure that Brodie would return and had managed to persuade Holly to trust his belief. 'He'll be just away on an adventure,' he had told her. 'Let's not tell the others just yet.'

Holly hated telling lies, but she was so worried for Jock's status in the community that she kept up the story that Brodie was inside the burrow with haggis flu. Everyone kept away from them because haggis flu could last for months and was pretty nasty on the nostrils and the throat, taking away their ability to sing for months on end. Jock and Holly kept inside too, worrying by day and searching by night when everybody was asleep. Apart from tonight – they were so tired. So empty with Brodie missing.

Jock blinked the tiredness from his eyes and surveyed the scene that unfolded in front of him. Snoring haggises lay sprawled at the opening of each burrow – some further out into the open – in a deep, deep sleep. The snoring, louder than usual, began to reduce as some haggises stirred from their spell-induced sleep.

'Get back inside,' Jock hissed to Holly. He knew the scene well. Holly didn't. Danger had been right inside Drumdrui. Right at their burrows, and it had taken all of the haggises to reduce whatever it was to heather.

'What's up?' asked Holly, worried by Jock's urgency.

Jock was quick to respond. 'I think Stan McGillis is on the prowl. I'm just going to take a look for Brodie again – alone this time. You're tired – you need to get some more sleep. Whilst

Stan McGillis won't really suspect me roaming around the hillside at this hour of darkness, he will suspect you.'

Relieved that Holly didn't witness the sleeping haggises, Jock started to poke around the centre of Drumdrui to find the piece of heather. There must be one, he thought as he searched behind trees and stones, but he found nothing, apart from an unusual set of footprints. He looked around. There were no other footprints leading to them or away from them – how had the enemy got there? He looked into the sky – maybe some sort of bird had landed.

As the haggises began to stir, Jock took off up the hillside towards Darmaeddie Loch. None of them would remember what the danger was and he had to leave it that way. He would look for the heather in the morning. Whatever it was, it would emerge soon – hopefully as friend and not foe.

Jock arrived at the shores of the loch. The splashes of water over the pebbles told him that something had emerged from the water recently – he was sure of that. He looked around, but only saw haggis footprints in the fading snow. Nothing out of the ordinary. Just his footprints from pacing the shore night after night looking for Brodie. A sudden splash caused him to jump back in fright.

CHAPTER NINE

Big Bag and Knobbly Knees

Lunch at Skibo Castle was unlike anything that Erin had ever been witness to before. It wasn't the large dining room that amazed her with its walls heavily lined with old oak paintings. Nor was it the long table brimming with the finest of foods that she had ever seen. Nor was it the famous celebrities buzzing around her. Or the wealth of jewellery that clung to their skin.

Erin stood open-mouthed, amazed at the number of goblins, heather-pixies, trolls, boglouts and other weird looking creatures that were crawling all over the table, smelling the food as they salivated over it. They knew that they couldn't take anything because if they did, the food would be noticed moving across the table. They were there to have some fun and pick the crumbs from the floor and take food from the table after everyone had left, but just now, it was party time.

Some trolls dipped their tongues into the soup and the relish dishes. Some faeries licked at the sugar in the sugar bowl. One boglout sneezed all over it and splattered the sugar with mucus and some black bits. Erin grimaced at the thought and coughed a retch when she realised what the mysterious black bits were she had often found in sugar bowls, butter dishes and some salads.

One young heather-pixie broke free from his parents and hovered over the large terrine of Scotch broth. He grinned devilishly before lowering himself into the dish, just dipping his bottom into the broth and no more. His face turned red as it puffed up like a balloon. The broth bubbled slightly and the pixie giggled childishly as he bum-burped the alphabet into it. Erin groaned miserably. It gave a complete new meaning to alphabet soup.

Once the pixie's parents noticed what he was doing, he was

dragged away by his ear screaming and wailing as hard as his lungs would allow him. A large blob of broth was about to fall from his bottom onto the table, but his father briskly flew underneath and caught it in his mouth. They looked around to see if anyone had noticed. They hadn't – apart from an old man peering into the Scotch broth with interest. He turned and spoke to the elderly woman sitting to his right.

'Did you see that Scotch broth move? It's alive, I tell you. It's alive.' He raised his glass of Glen Morangie to her before gulping it down.

The woman peered into the broth, but she didn't see it move. She looked at the old man with disgust as the ghastly smell from the young heather-pixie finally flowed in her direction.

'No,' she replied abruptly, raising a napkin to her nose. 'It's not alive, but something smells as though it just died!' She screwed up her nose at the old man and turned away from him. 'Smelly, drunken old fool,' she muttered to her friend.

Erin closed her eyes slowly and shook her head. Life would never be the same for her after seeing this.

The noise of the faeries was much greater than the buzz of the people chattering. Brodie looked around in amazement. He could hear and see everything that they were doing, but not one person, apart from Erin, even knew that they were there. Some goblins had to side step the people to avoid being kicked. Dozens of heather-pixies flew around women's heads to get a better view of the jewellery they were wearing, sneezing violently as they breathed in the heavy concoction of hairsprays and perfumes.

'Look at that beautiful diamond on that one there,' gasped one young heather-pixie as she fluttered around the young American lady sitting across from Erin. 'I'm going to sleep next to that tonight.' The heather-pixie sighed delightfully at the thought of spending the night with such an expensive, and glittering diamond. Large diamonds like that were the source of eternal youth to many of the faeries.

The creatures arrived at the castle with plenty of luggage, but most didn't contain a change of clothes. They were taken to hide away any scraps of food that fell onto the floor, or that were about to be discarded, or that were sitting out and could be taken when nobody was watching. They didn't regard taking food as stealing. Stealing was a very punishable crime in their world. They would play with jewellery and clothes and toys belonging to the guests at the castle, but they would never steal them. The rule was that whatever got left behind by the guests they could claim it as their own. So, most would deliberately hide things and claim them when they were left behind by the guests. That way they couldn't be accused of stealing.

Brodie's stomach rumbled as the aroma of rich food wafted past his nostrils. Erin heard the rumbles and grabbed an apple, orange and banana from the bowl of fruit, stuffed a few chocolate chip cookies in her bag and asked to be excused. 'I'd like to explore the castle if I may?' she asked her mother.

Brenda frowned and signalled for her to stay where she was.

'Yes – she can roam free if she would like to. She'll be bored with this lot,' interrupted a kilted waiter who had just placed a large silver tray of warm bread rolls down on the table. Erin smiled gratefully at the young man, grabbed two rolls and sloped out of the room with Brodie slung over her back before her mother could say anything else.

Booger had been disgusted at the commotion of the creatures around the table and their greed. He emerged from the dark corner where he had hidden himself and followed on behind her. He hated noise. If that racket was going on in his forest … well … then he stopped himself from any more nasty thoughts.

Brodie looked back at the table as Erin left the busy dining room. Lunch had begun and everyone had started to eat. The floor was littered with a variety of creatures as they scrambled around the chairs catching any crumbs. Some ate them straight away. Some had their luggage with them to store it in, so there were plenty of bags with their mouths wide open, taking instructions from their masters as to which direction to run in. As soon as something was caught, the bag would snap shut and burp satisfyingly before repositioning themselves for the next crumb.

Brodie looked across to Dion Cameron who was smiling warmly. She stared straight at his eyes. A pale white glow surrounded her. A giddy feeling washed over Brodie as he began to drift in and out of consciousness. Everything became misty and the dark image that had dominated his dreams before seemed to be getting stronger through the mist as the white glow weakened. Brodie felt his strength gradually slip away as the dark image engulfed the mist.

Erin roamed the large oak-lined corridors poking her head into rooms and studying the stern faces in oversized portraits that hung from the walls.

'They all look so angry,' said the ghillie dhu as he followed Erin closely.

Erin looked around her and smiled, then slid the rucksack from her shoulders. 'Time for a leg stretch Brodie.'

Brodie felt weak as he crawled out of the bag and almost went back into it when he saw Booger.

'Hi Brodie, my friend – I missed you!' The ghillie dhu flapped around Brodie like an excited puppy dog.

Brodie tripled up the corridor to gain as much distance from him as possible. 'Aw, get lost Booger! You're just one big pain.'

'I thought we were friends ... I need to help you. I will help you!' Although his eyes seemed a little saddened by Brodie's rejection, his voice remained full of determination and sincerity.

Just then, one of the large oak doors further down the corridor burst open and a gust of strong cold wind rushed against them. Erin and Booger turned and stared sharply at the door. Brodie tripled back up the corridor and slipped in behind Erin's legs. They all stood, watching, waiting, hardly breathing. Brodie's heart beat loudly in his ears. The seconds ticked by but nobody emerged from the room. They all shuffled quietly towards the open door and stopped when they heard small voices.

'Hurry up you pile of useless carpet fluff. Before we miss out on all the fun of raiding the rooms when everyone is stuffing their faces. Now come on will you!'

'Nag, nag, nag. Moan, moan, moan. I'll be there in a minute – I'm looking at the pretty pictures – OK?'

A very large, very worn carpetbag stood just beyond Brodie gazing up at the large portraits displayed around the walls in the room. His eyes blinked slowly and intelligently as he looked at each one in turn, absorbing every detail. He took a sly look at his master and then took a long, slow look back at the portrait. He wasn't interested in the artwork at all – he seemed more interested in winding up the elf who was hurling insults at him.

'I said get a move on dirt bag! I want to get the goodies before the rest of them do! I've got customers to satisfy.' Knobbly Knees, spat ferociously at the bag. His eyebrows hung low over his eyes. 'I'm going to count to three and …'

'Ok, ok, don't get your knickers in a twist master oh Lord and Mighty, I'm coming, I'm coming! Gee wiz and bang – anyone would think you were in a rush. And by the way, the name's Big Bag, not Dirt Bag – Puke Breath!'

'I am in a rush you old bag. Now get a move on will you!'

Big Bag laughed slyly. The gold ring threaded through his nose glinted as he twitched his moustache from side to side. He had managed to severely upset Knobbly Knees. Mission accomplished. The wise old bag knew not to push him too far for fear of being banished to the bag retirement home long before his time. Although his master knew that he was a pretty rare bag and to find another like him would take a long time and a lot of training – so he knew that he was quite safe. Their relationship was one of a love hate relationship – they loved to hate one another. They'd been together for decades now and Big Bag was fairly confident that he wouldn't trade him in … not just yet. He chuckled quietly to himself as he whizzed past Brodie towards his master. It was like he hadn't even seen Brodie.

The skinny elf scowled at the over-sized bag through hardened, pink eyes. He had two gold earrings threaded through each pointed ear and his long, slightly bearded chin drew attention to his even longer, thinner nose. He was said to be the gypsy of all elves. A sailor-type scarf hung around his long neck and a small muslin satchel was slung around his waist. He was dressed from head to toe in well-worn, frayed muslin. Even his pointed elf shoes were made of muslin and tied securely around his ankles to avoid them slipping off when he was forcing himself through the narrowest of gaps to escape.

His most prominent features were his namesake knobbly knees. Even through the muslin cloth, they glowed like red-hot embers. Some say they were his most precious assets – that they led him to his treasures.

He had just found something interesting and the flesh-coloured skin on his face creased with dozens of small lines as he grinned triumphantly. 'Here, catch this,' he instructed to his trusty old bag.

The large bag immediately opened his mouth and ran towards the elf to catch whatever he was throwing at him. A large vase hurtled through the air and the bag widened his mouth around it, swallowed it and snapped his mouth shut. For a moment, the carpetbag swelled to the size of the vase. After he let out an enjoyable burp, the vase shape disappeared and he returned to his normal size. Brodie stared on silently.

Booger leaned in and whispered cautiously. 'That's Big Bag and Knobbly Knees. The most notorious thieves in our world.'

They all watched the leggy elf leave the room and make his way up the stairs towards the guest rooms. The muslin cloth was wrapped around his legs like bandages. His legs looked more like two pieces of rope hanging from his hips with large knots in the middle. His arms were much the same with large knobbly elbows. Only, they didn't glow red like his knees did.

Big Bag tripped up the stairs after the elf mumbling his discontent at how full he was feeling already and they hadn't even started yet. He let out another burp as he made room for whatever else Knobbly Knees was going to throw at him. They certainly weren't a match made in heaven.

Most other bags obeyed their masters and followed on behind faithfully, not allowing anyone to steal them, and never back chatting their master. The bags always hovered at an exact distance from the ground and from their masters. When they weren't required, their masters would simply instruct the bags to "stay", and no matter what happened or who tried to move them, they wouldn't move until their masters gave a new instruction. Nobody could undo the bond between master and bag. It remained faithful to the end. Although, how Knobbly Knees had managed to endure Big Bag's tantrums for so long, nobody understood.

Brodie chuckled heartily at them but Booger looked on gravely.

'What's wrong?' Brodie asked as he noticed the concern in the ghillie dhu's face.

Booger eventually responded when the duo were out of sight. 'I don't know – something smells a bit fishy.'

Brodie looked around him. 'There's no water here – where are the fish? I don't smell anything.'

Erin laughed at Brodie's innocence as he tripled around the hall looking for fish.

'No you fruitcake. There are no fish. What I mean is that something doesn't seem right ... with those two.'

'In what way?' asked Erin, lowering her voice and bending down to the ghillie dhu's level. Brodie moved in closer and his eyes widened with curiosity.

Booger looked at them both with pride. They were being nice to him and wanted to listen to what he had to say. He'd never experienced that before and he was really beginning to like it. A warmth ran through his heart sending him into a dizzy pleasure.

'Go on, tell us.' Brodie was becoming impatient.

'Well … it's just that …' He paused for a few moments.

'It's just what?' Erin asked persuasively.

'Wherever they appear, there's sure to be trouble. Knobbly Knees only steals to order and these days, he only does it for somebody big and powerful. He's very expensive to hire – the best in the business.'

'What could he possibly steal from here for your world?'

The ghillie dhu turned his stare to Brodie. Erin turned and looked at Brodie as well.

Brodie stood in silence and looked from Erin to Booger, watching the fear run through their eyes. 'What's everyone looking so worried about? Anybody gets in my way and I'll turn them into heather. Have you all forgotten that?'

Erin smiled gently at Brodie's surge of eagerness. 'You couldn't turn it on for Ly Erg – remember? He didn't make you angry or frightened enough. What if that happens again?'

'Yeah, but I let him have my smell – that sorted him out. Where there's a will, there's a way,' said Brodie assertively, raising his top lip like a horse to reveal his yellow teeth.

Erin screwed up her nose as she remembered the powerful odour that Brodie had used against Ly Erg. She smiled thoughtfully. The only real cure for a midge-less picnic in the Scottish Highlands was to make sure they had a haggis with them – like that would really happen!

The ghillie dhu lowered his voice. 'We just have to be

careful.' His eyes pulsed from green to luminous green and the moss on his body quivered as he worried about the safety of his new friends.

They soon forgot about the quarrelling duo and made their way through corridors, drifting in and out of the different rooms. Some were brightly coloured; others were less colourful and full of large wooden furniture. Once or twice Brodie was shoved in behind a door or into a cupboard when somebody passed by them or came out of one of the rooms, but luckily, nobody caught sight of him.

They climbed the large staircase to the next floor and wandered along a similar corridor. A door to one of the bedrooms had been left open and Brodie tripled into it. The room was so large that it dwarfed the huge four-poster bed in it. Heavy curtains framed the tall windows, and small lamps dotted around the room gave it a warm, winter's glow.

'Quick – under the bed!' ordered Booger. 'It's Big Bag and Knobbly Knees – I hear them outside in the corridor.

Brodie tripled around the room three times in a frenzied panic. Erin stood at the bed holding the valance sheet up. 'Come on you silly haggis – over here!'

Brodie ran towards her and crashed under the bed. Erin and Booger just got themselves tucked under in time. All three of them watched secretly through an opening in the heavily embroidered valance sheet.

'Will you get a move on you old bag. I've got work to do!'

'Look, I'm hurrying as quickly as I can – but with all this stuff you've given me to carry, how can you expect me to move any faster?' Big Bag hiccupped painfully. Sweat was running down his nose and dripping onto the floor. 'I need a rest – I'll just set down here for a little while. You go and have a look around – maybe you'll find what you're looking for.' The bulging bag stopped hovering and lowered himself to the floor with a clatter. He wheezed and panted as he took time to get his breath back. 'No more, please, until I've emptied this lot.'

Knobbly Knees threw a look of scorn at the bag as it lay in a collapsed heap on the floor. 'You're a lazy good for nothing … why, when I get enough time to train a new bag, I'm going to retire you – gladly!'

'Good – and maybe my new master will have a bit more respect for me you long streak of misery. Maybe I'll get times when I can curl up in front of a nice warm fire and take a break.'

Big Bag lay on the floor looking hurt and miserable whilst the knobbly-knee'd elf roamed around the room looking for treasures. He was careful to set everything back the way it was – he had to make sure that nobody would suspect him being there. He was light on his feet and light with his fingers too. No wonder he was so sought after by the villains. He was such a professional.

The law was that he couldn't take anything that was in its rightful place. He could only take it if it had been carelessly discarded and left behind, but he was a low life who ignored the rules. His pay packet was all that he was interested in. He busied himself around the dressing table and admired the sparkling jewellery. Then his keen eye spied a bright red ruby ring tucked in behind the mirror. A sly grin twisted his face as he slipped it into the muslin satchel that hung from his bony hips. 'This one isn't for Big Bag,' he muttered and continued poking around the room. His knees began to glow bright red. He was getting dangerously close to the bed. Booger had to divert him.

'Wait here,' he whispered, before springing out from under the bed.

Erin tightened her grip around Brodie.

'Long time no see, Knobbly Knees!'

The skinny elf pivoted on his heels and faced the green ghillie dhu. His pink eyes stared hard into Booger's green eyes. Then he let out a grunt.

'So, you finally got out of that forest of yours. Who's

running it now?' His voice clinked like a rattling chain.

'Gertruda, most likely,' Booger replied, stepping casually away from the bed so that the elf didn't notice Brodie. 'So, you're having a clearout in here are you? Who're you stealing for this time?' The ghillie dhu's voice turned hard and the skin around his pointed nose twitched nervously.

'That be none of your booger-nose business, slime ball. Now get lost – this is my patch.'

'Have you even paid to get in here? You're just fleecing the rooms before any of the rest get a look in – and they've paid for the privilege. How'd you slip by the army of boglouts?'

'Look – first come first served as far as I'm concerned. I know a few of the boglouts, so it's not a problem for me.' A deep chuckle played around in the bottom of his throat as he stroked his chin with his famously nimble fingers. 'What brings you here? Didn't think that a place like this needed any snotbuckets. You've probably upset everyone's holiday by being here – why don't you just skip off back to your damp little forest.'

Steam rose from the ghillie dhu's small, pointed ears as Knobbly Knees continued to insult him. He raised his arms towards the elf and they grew in length, ready to snare him.

Knobbly Knees continued to stare back at him and he grinned slowly. 'So … you want to know what I've come here for then? Show him Big Bag!' The elf took one step forward and pushed the ghillie dhu hard in the chest. The ghillie dhu fell backwards and Big Bag was right behind him with his mouth wide open. It took two seconds for the bag to swallow him.

Brodie watched Booger's two green shoes try to kick free from the bag's grasp, but one after the other, they disappeared into the bag's mouth. There was a bit of a struggle inside the bag and Booger's muffled cries could be heard, but they soon disappeared after the bag let out a very large burp. He was gone.

'Well done there Big Bag. Now – off to Gertruda with the

little snotbucket – mission accomplished. There's a big fat bonus waiting for us. She's right – she said it would be easy to get him since that furry haggis thing messed with his mind. He's like putty in my hands ... putty. Ha, ha, ha ...' Knobbly Knees drifted out of the room and Big Bag zipped in behind him, following on with a smug smile on his face. He must've paused once or twice to look at something because the elf shouted back to him to hurry up.

Once the voices had completely disappeared, Brodie crawled out from under the bed. He sat down heavily and began to sob and wail like a dozen bagpipers were being strangled.

'Ssshhh, or you'll be discovered,' said Erin in a hushed voice. 'Gertruda must be worried that Booger would help us. He was our only hope of getting inside her mind.'

Brodie tried to be comforted by Erin, but his grief was too much. 'I didn't even really like him – but I must've because I feel so sad. I think I'm going to miss him.' He continued to wail as Erin picked him up and tucked him back into the rucksack. He didn't know how to stop his wailing – it just flowed, and flowed, and flowed.

'Brodie – if you don't want to be turned into a haggis platter – I'd suggest you pull yourself together – NOW! Crying is not going to do you or anyone else any good. Get a grip of yourself now – we've got to get back to the forest – Gertruda's forest.'

Brodie stopped immediately and stared up into Erin's blue eyes. They were full of determination, but there was fear in them as well. The last time she was in the forest, Gertruda almost killed her.

CHAPTER TEN

McCloud, Mildred and Charlie Boo

Brodie's anger boiled as Erin made her way down the stairs. Gertruda had to be stopped and Brodie was ready to battle with her to free the haggises once and for all. He looked at the portraits on the wall flashing past as Erin made her way along the corridor towards the dining room. They seemed to be glaring at him – did nobody smile? He recalled the painting of Alexander McHaggerty that Gertruda had enshrined in her broken down cottage back in the forest glade. His eyes had looked so real and full of hatred. He shuddered.

'Oh there you are dear. What a beautiful lunch you missed – such wonderful food.' Erin's mother gushed over the fine details of what she had eaten. 'We must leave now in daylight. Don't want to be driving through mist in the dark, do we?'

Brodie's thoughts drifted back to the Scotch Mist. It would be gone now that Booger had been captured – it must've been him they were after – not Brodie. Gertruda obviously needed the ghillie dhu for her plan and they must have been trying to get him themselves. Once back in the forest, Brodie felt sure that the ghillie dhu would revert to his old ways and would soon forget any friendship he had tried to forge with them.

After a swathe of goodbyes, hugs, kisses and promises to email Dion Cameron, Erin and her parents climbed into the car. Goblins, boglouts, heather-pixies, elves, and other weird creatures and their luggage continued to check into the castle as another batch checked out. It was business as usual for them.

'I slept with the big diamond last night and I feel fifty years younger already,' cooed a small heather-pixie as she flew down the front steps with a group of her friends. Her translucent wings buzzed gently as she hovered around and welcomed the new batch of holidaymakers. 'Trixie has already taken ownership of the diamond for tonight so you lot won't get a chance to sleep on it. Oh, but there are plenty of others – so get in there quick, girls. I feel just wonderful. Just wonderful!' The heather-pixie sighed contentedly, and somersaulted three times in the air before flying south. Her heather-clad bag somersaulted three times and zipped off after her, looking a bit dizzy and somewhat fatter than when she had arrived two days ago with her master.

Erin snapped her seatbelt on and looked at the empty seat next to her where Booger had sat on the way to Skibo Castle. She had begun to get used to him and missed him in a strange kind of way, but he would be back with his old cronies and no doubt causing a nuisance of himself once again.

Brodie squealed sharply when somebody knocked fiercely on the car window. Erin tried to mimic the squeal so that her parents thought it was her. She stared at Dion Cameron who was standing outside of the car waving frantically to them.

Brenda pressed the button on the door to lower the window.

'I've just been told that the road is closed at the end of the drive due to a jack-knifed lorry. Hit something in the mist, apparently. She pointed down the long drive. 'Look – the mist is coming this way.'

Brodie groaned miserably.

'I've already spoken to the manager. You can be my guests for the night. The staff are making up rooms for you and getting some supplies together. Please – do come in.' Her warm smile and sparkling eyes begged them to accept her offer.

Brenda and Ralph had no hesitation in accepting the kind offer – a chance to stay in Skibo Castle for free! They thanked the Canadian star and said they would be straight in after they had parked the car and made some quick phone calls on their mobile phones. The car tyres crunched over the snow as Ralph reversed back into the space that he had just pulled out of.

Erin's heart raced as she watched the mist roll up the driveway – the most fearsome of the mist-spirits with the large fangs and three eyes was leading an army of mist-spirits. A small, yellow ball of mist tumbled up behind them. A female mist-spirit swished in beside the leader with her arms folded across her chest, her eyes glowing a rich purple colour.

'Yes dear, we can hardly see out of the car because the mist is so thick.' Brenda chatted freely into her phone. 'Could be here for a while.' Both Brenda and Ralph continued to chat into their phones, unaware of the mist-spirits attaching themselves to their car.

'Can you get in there?' asked McCloud as he pushed his large nose onto the car windscreen. Glistening saliva dripped down his two fangs.

'What do you think I am – a contortionist?' said Mildred as she tied herself into a knot and then snapped out if it like a cracked whip.

'Well, we have got to think of something Mildred. Charlie Boo – will you stop messing around!' The small yellow ball of mist flew in and out of the mist-spirits, banging into some of them, pinching the bottoms of others and screeching in their ears. He giggled tirelessly.

Mildred looked at the young mist-spirit sympathetically. 'Oh McCloud – don't be so hard on him, he's just … happy. He has joined us so young … give him a chance.' The deep scars on her face sparkled in the mist as she smiled back at McCloud, but he didn't return the smile. He growled fiercely.

'That idiot's always happy – even with the thought of Gertruda reigning over us. He's driving me nuts, I tell you. Nuts!'

'Well, maybe you should take some of whatever he has taken to be happy. You're such a miserable old grouch, McCloud. We've got a mission to do and the sooner we get it done the sooner we can rest in peace again. But we can't get it done with you constantly moaning and griping at everyone.' Mildred flicked her eyes up and swished her misty hair back.

The large mist-spirit glared at Mildred as she hovered beside him with her arms folded and her nose primly stuck up in the air. Two striped worms wiggled above each eye. Her red pointed lips revealed a row of rotting teeth as she spoke in a high, who-do-you-think-you-are pitch. She circled the car again to see if there was any way in.

'It's no use – we're locked out.'

The red eye in the middle of McCloud's bluey-white face pulsated and twitched angrily. 'Will you lot PLEASE be quiet – I'm trying to think here! Unless any of you has a better idea?' McCloud looked around at the hundreds of mist-spirits that had been summoned to help him. They stopped chattering and practicing their really bad jokes and turned to stare at him, blinking silently. Hovering even quieter.

McCloud breathed in deeply before he continued. 'I, more than anyone, want to get back to my rest. We will do the job – no excuses.' He delivered his words in a very powerful and calculated voice, which oozed authority. All of the mist-spirits nodded in agreement and began to circle the car again, this time being much quieter.

McCloud stared in through the window at Erin. 'We've just simply got to complete our mission. I can't bear the thought of …'

DOUFF!

Charlie Boo, laughed uncontrollably as he bumped hard into McCloud. McCloud's head squashed against the windscreen and his large body rammed into it. Charlie Boo bounced from McCloud onto the roof of the car and then somersaulted and circled in the air like a firefly. His eyes continued to rotate in opposite directions, only stopping occasionally when he was lining himself up for another tumble run. He didn't care who he bumped into or how much it hurt. It was just pure fun to him – wasn't that what life was all about?

A single loud pop jolted Brodie as McCloud popped his head back out of his misty body. He was even angrier than ever. The other mist-spirits sank back into the mist. All that Erin could see were dozens of faded eyes blinking quietly from the mist. McCloud's body became bolder and less mist-like as he squared up and searched for Charlie Boo.

'BOO!' shouted Charlie Boo mischievously as he crept up beside the large mist-spirit. McCloud shot up into the air with fright and bashed his head on a large, very stout mist-spirit above him. He hovered, dazed, for a few moments and then slumped to the ground. A loud gasp filtered around the mist-spirits as they faded back into the mist.

'Sorry old man,' said Charlie Boo in a half-hearted attempt to apologise to him. He just didn't know what a nuisance he was or what trouble meant. It was all fun to him. 'I was only playing – didn't think that you'd be so easily scared.' Try as he might, he couldn't contain the broad smile that eventually split his face in two, three and four pieces. He laughed so loud that Erin looked to her parents to see if they had heard him, but they were both still talking into their mobile phones, unaware of the spirits outside the car.

A loud grumbling noise, like thunder, echoed around the sky as McCloud's anger increased. After dislodging his two fangs from the wet ground, he pulled himself up slowly and strongly and gripped Charlie Boo by the shoulder. The rumble of thunder continued to grow louder the angrier McCloud became.

'Mildred – will you get this piece of yellow muck out of my face – he's going to ruin the whole plan!'

Mildred didn't appear.

McCloud pushed his face into Charlie Boo's young face, but the yellow spirit simply licked his face and returned a warm and friendly smile. Another rumble of thunder echoed around the skies. McCloud gripped Charlie Boo's shoulder firmly and catapulted him into the air so hard that he looked like a flash of lightening through the sky.

'Ooh, thunder and lightening. I think we'd better get inside now,' cooed Brenda after she ended her phone call. 'Did you see the lightening … unusual for this time of year … and in the mist ...'

Erin unfastened her seatbelt and waited for her mother to open the door before she opened her door. She had to stay close to them – she had no idea what the spirits would do to her.

Brodie watched from the depths of the rucksack. Erin tucked herself between her mother and father as they walked up the grand steps once again. They passed by the boglouts' check in desk at the bottom of the stairs. One family of goblins was nervously asking for a refund because they didn't want to stay around where there was going to be trouble.

'We came here to avoid the Scotch Mist. Now it's here – we want to go home. We want our money back – we're not staying here to watch someone's blood spill.'

'Ever thought that it could be yours?' the boglout spat as he sat behind an old oak desk stacking up thistle pennies. His brown eyes and teeth sparkled devilishly as he refused to give a refund. 'Maybe if you go, the mist will follow. You know they won't give up until they've achieved their mission. No refunds. So, what is it – stay or go?' The boglout sniggered viciously at the goblins as they stood anxiously at the desk, just managing to side step Brenda's feet as she almost ploughed through them.

Brodie didn't like what he was seeing. A deep growl rumbled in his throat as he spoke through the mesh of the bag. 'Give them a refund or you'll be like your cousins were – a piece of lucky white heather!'

The sleazy boglouts looked up at the bag and saw Brodie's blue eyes staring back at them. Erin turned and glared down at them as well. The boglouts conferred briefly and hesitated, before reluctantly handing the thistle pennies back to the goblins. 'You'll pay for this Brodie McHaggis – for sure you will, FOR SURE!'

The goblins took their thistle pennies and scuttled off into the mist, muttering their appreciation to Brodie without daring to look back.

McCloud puffed up beside Erin. His eyes blinked one after the other and his middle eye glowed scarlet-red. Erin punched at the mist-spirit, but her hand went straight through him. An empty coldness entered her body as she felt herself being drawn further and further into the soul-less mist.

Brodie gasped at the sudden coldness that ran through his bones, making them ache. His teeth chattered. It was a coldness like no other, but it went as soon as Erin snapped her hand back from the mist. It had turned blue and was covered in small beads of ice. As she looked into McCloud's eyes, a shiver ran down her spine. Brodie felt the shiver as it passed by him. Erin gasped and ran inside to the safety of her parents.

Erin was too exhausted to appreciate the magnificent beauty of the room that she had been given to stay in. She had immediately fallen asleep when the softness of the enormous bed had cocooned her tired body. Brodie lay sprawled out beside her, examining the large tartan canopy over the bed and enjoying the warmth and comfort. The luxurious quilt was so thick that he was almost buried in it.

Eventually becoming bored of looking at the canopy, he climbed along the soft quilt, jumped onto the oak chest at the end of the bed, and jumped onto the deep piled carpet to explore the rest of the room. It was truly outstanding. Large lamps lit three of the corners and an arrangement of plants surrounded a table lamp in the other corner. They gave the room a warm and cosy glow. Brodie looked back at Erin, sleeping like a princess. The bedroom door clicked open. He ducked in behind the plants.

'Erin looks so tired for someone so young,' whispered Brenda as she crept into the room with Ralph. Two goblins darted into the room after them, followed by two pieces of luggage obediently following on behind them.

'Over here – look – we'll have those chairs for tonight,' shouted one of the goblins as he ran towards the two easy chairs just under the window. 'I don't think we'll get much loot in this room, but it'll be quiet.' They jumped up into the chairs and their bags parked themselves under them, beginning to unpack.

'You know,' Brenda mused, craning her neck to absorb the full beauty of the lavish room. 'I think this room is even bigger than ours. Wow … what luxury. How the other half live,' she sighed pensively.

'Look at those dark rings under her eyes.' Ralph pressed the back of his hand against Erin's pale forehead. 'I hope she isn't coming down with something.'

'She has been acting rather strangely these past few days. I can't quite put my finger on what it is – but she's even been speaking to herself. Are we neglecting her? Remember when she used to speak to that old gnome that Rose has in her garden – you know, the ugly one that keeps disappearing. I think she used to call him Gnogard or something like that. She was just four years old then and I thought she'd grown out of that imaginary friends stuff. Do you think she's lonely? Should we do something?'

Ralph looked at Erin sleeping peacefully and he rested his eyes on the black rucksack tucked in against the side of the bed. 'You don't think that she's got anything to do with that gnome going missing? Is that what she's carrying around with her the whole time?'

Brenda's eyes fell on the rucksack too and she stared at it in silence. 'We'll talk to her about it tomorrow.'

'Don't you think we should take a look?'

Brenda hesitated for a moment and then shook her head. 'No, it would be dishonest. We'll talk to her tomorrow.'

They left the room quietly. Brodie let out a huge sigh after the door clicked shut and emerged from behind the plants.

The two goblins shrieked and ran around the room wondering how to get away from Brodie before he turned them into heather.

Brodie sighed again. 'I don't want to harm you. If you leave me alone, then I'll leave you alone – simple as that. I'd prefer to be your friends.'

The goblins weren't listening. They gathered up their belongings, threw them into their bags and ran for the door. One goblin gave a leg up to the other to open the door and they slipped out, unnoticed by anyone else and the bags followed on behind them, just as scared.

Brodie sat in the middle of the floor, lonely, upset and hungry. His stomach growled loudly. He hadn't eaten much all day. His loneliness was soon forgotten as he searched Erin's rucksack for food. Nothing, not even a crumb. He looked around the room until his gaze rested on the plants in the corner.

***

Brodie pressed in close to Erin as they looked out of the window at the mist-spirits.

'They're still here,' he sighed, feeling less bored now that Erin was awake. They watched the spirits together as some guarded the window, some played a sort of tag game, and others drifted aimlessly, crying about something and holding their heads in their hands. Brodie told Erin what her parents had said about Gnogard.

'Gnogard? You mean … I used to talk to him when I was a wee lass?' Erin scratched her forehead trying to remember one conversation that she'd had with him.

'That's what your mother said. They thought you were talking to yourself. Did you ever see anyone else – anything in the forest?'

Erin shook her head in amazement. 'I don't remember any of it, and why can I see them for what they are now? What's changed?' She looked at Brodie and her eyes shone brightly. 'It's because of you!'

Brodie picked at the skin around his talons and frowned.

'You're real ... but you're not.'

Brodie still didn't understand what she was babbling on about.

'Well – you're meant to be a myth, but you aren't – you're very real. You can see into their world, and because I've seen you … and the Loch Ness Monster … well, I've obviously opened my mind and I can see everything else. Just like young children do.'

As Brodie shook his head at Erin, his long fluted nose waggled from side to side. 'Oh – and your mother thinks that you're carrying Gnogard around in that bag of yours. Thinks you've got something to do with him disappearing … again.'

Erin coughed a laugh. 'Well Brodie, in a way, I have got something to do with him disappearing. I think we need to find him – I've just remembered something about when I used to talk to him. He owes me big time.' A wide smile divided her pale face as she placed her hand on the windowpane and stared beyond it into the mist.

CHAPTER ELEVEN

The Jokers

Brodie pressed his nose against the window and ran his tongue along the glass as he watched the mist-spirits. He pushed four of his toe-like fingers up into his nostrils to block them, and blew hard through his nose so that his nostrils inflated like balloons. Then he crossed his eyes and stuck out his tongue.

The spirits hovered outside, watching him grimly. Not a smile. Not a twitch. Just scowls. They didn't find him funny.

Brodie blew so hard that his fingers shot out of his nostrils and released a large bagpipe sound. It was so loud that it hurt his ears and he knocked himself backwards onto the floor. When he climbed back up to the windowsill, the mist-spirits were gone. Then slowly, eyes started appearing out of the mist, followed by their bodies as they edged back cautiously.

Brodie smiled widely. 'So, you're scared of the haggis sound, eh?' He chuckled and started to chant through his nose. Some spirits shot up into the sky and banged into one another and others just popped like balloons bursting.

'Jings McCrackerty – they're a bunch of wuusses!' Brodie laughed loudly and never noticed the door opening behind him. He continued to laugh and blow his nose so hard that his own ears started to ring. He hadn't had this much fun in a long time. He fell back onto the chair and waggled his three feet in the air, laughing freely. As he looked up to the ceiling, two large blue eyes stared down at him.

'Uh oh.' He stopped moving, his heart barely beating.

'Uh oh indeed. You're just lucky that it was me, Brodie McHaggis. You can be heard all over the castle – Mum thought that it was the pipers practicing for tonight's dinner. I knew it was you and came back straight away. You have got to be careful!'

Brodie sprung onto his feet and climbed back up to the windowsill. 'Why don't we just go and ask them what they want? See if they can find Gnogard for us.'

'You know, that may not be such a bad idea,' Erin mused as she listened to the muffled whines of the mist-spirits through the glass.

'Come on then.' Brodie jumped down to the floor and dived headfirst into the rucksack. 'Let's go!'

Brodie plugged his ears with his taloned fingers to drown out the noise of the mist-spirits. They surrounded Erin as soon as she stepped outside of the castle, screaming and shouting at her and repeating their terrible jokes in her face. They laughed insanely before telling a joke and laughed even more insanely after they'd told it to Erin.

'Knock, knock Erin.'

Erin sidestepped the mist-spirit, but another one got in her way.

'He said knock, knock, Erin. It's rude not to answer him.' The long thin mist-spirit laughed hard.

'Ok, ok. Who's there?'

'Boo! It's us – silly old you. Why, can't you see us? Haar, haar, haar.' And so the jokes continued.

'Why did the mist-spirit cross the road, Erin?'

Erin stuck her head down and ploughed through the mist with her fingers jammed in her ears, but she could still hear them. It was like they had entered her head. It pounded with bad jokes and irritating laughter.

'Don't know? Give up? Why, to get to the other side, Erin. Ahaaa, haa, haa.'

No matter where Erin turned, there were dozens more mist-spirits willing to unleash their jokes on her. It was the most depressing thing that she had ever had to deal with. Every time she ploughed through a spirit, the cold dampness entered her bones and made her feel soul-less so she tried outwitting them. She pretended to go one way and then skipped back the other way. It worked for a while, but they soon cottoned on to her plan.

'Ha, ha, ha. And how do you make a snooker table laugh? Want to know Erin? Ha, ha, ha.'

'That will do McMuster. None of those jokes to a minor please – now shoo!' Mildred waved her willowy arms at the fat mist-spirit and he scuttled off. She folded her arms and hovered in front of Erin, disapprovingly.

'Not nice – is it?'

Erin stared at the worms wiggling above Mildred's eyes. She had the strangest eyebrows she had ever seen.

'Help us out and the Curse of the Scotch Mist will stop.'

'And if I don't?'

'Well ... you'll have a life of misery. You think these jokes are bad – they're being kind to you today Erin. It will get much, much worse. And when you've heard the same one fifty times in one hour – you'll want to help us.'

'No, it's not in here,' said Charlie Boo as he flew out of the hood on Erin's jacket. I'll try her pockets.' He laughed oddly and somersaulted from her hood down to her right pocket.

Brodie watched the spirits whiz by as they bombarded Erin. Erin ran towards the forest behind the castle. Every time she sliced through a mist-spirit, she weakened with cold and sorrow. Then she built up her speed again, until she punched through another one.

Brodie felt the same emptiness enter his body, but none of the spirits could forcefully stop them. He tried to use the Silent Protector on them, but when he realised that he couldn't, he knew that they weren't an immediate threat to him. He could only use it to save his life from something threatening him. Of course – a failsafe way by Noremac to make sure they didn't abuse their powers, but how could he use it to get away from their curse? He had to do something.

'Nothing Brodie. You can do absolutely nothing!' Charlie Boo popped out of Brodie's ear, kissed him on the nose and dissolved through the mesh in the rucksack. 'Help-ma-bob. I'm not going inside a haggis's head again – there's too much nonsense going on in there,' he chuckled boyishly. He launched himself towards Erin's ear, but she had it covered with her hand so he bounced back.

'Erin – I can't seem to use my powers – so it must mean that they're no immediate danger to me. They won't hurt you – find out what they want. Maybe they'll go away.' Brodie pressed his nose to the mesh and he breathed in the crisp winter air.

Erin stopped and challenged the mist-spirits. 'What is it you're after?'

McCloud whooshed in and hovered close to Erin. Mildred drifted in beside him and folded her arms boldly across her chest. Her purple eyes stared hard into Erin's eyes. Charlie Boo rolled in between them like a bowling ball and knocked them over.

'Wey hey! Hi Erin – want to play?' The small yellow spirit flickered in front of Erin like a dancing flame, his eyes rotating in opposite directions and his tongue waggling at the side of his mouth.

'Charlie Boo! What have we told you?' Mildred tidied her purple-tinged rats-tail hair and slapped the yellow spirit out of the way with the tail end of her body. 'Next time McCloud will kick you to the moon, not just to the other side of the loch.'

Charlie Boo giggled and rolled his eyes as he flew around the mist, bumping into other angry mist-spirits. 'The moon? The moon! Wow, it's my favourite colour – I'm going to the moon!' He whizzed up to one of the chimney pots on the castle and warmed his bottom.

McCloud drew himself back up to Erin. 'You know what we

want.'

Erin pulled the straps on her rucksack tightly and stuck her neck forward. 'Well if I knew what you wanted, why would I be asking? Huh? Talk about thick mist.'

McCloud stared strongly at Erin. Nobody insulted him.

Charlie Boo shouted down from the chimney pot. 'That little soldier's red hand – he wants the bit back that you have got. Ha, ha, ha, hee, hee, hee.'

Another mist-spirit flew up behind Charlie Boo, stuffed him down the chimney and sat himself on the chimney pot so that he couldn't get out.

McCloud turned back to Erin. 'Yes. We want that small piece of Ly Erg's hand.'

Brodie sighed with relief. First Booger, then Ly Erg. Nobody actually wanted him – maybe he could get back home without being noticed.

'Why?' asked Erin becoming very intrigued.

'Because ...,' he paused briefly. 'Because we need him to help us be free of Gertruda.' The spirit spoke slowly and purposefully.

Brodie became restless and Erin eventually slid the bag from her shoulders and let him out. The mist-spirits popped one by one until they had all disappeared.

'It's ok,' laughed Brodie as he felt a sense of power. 'I won't make any noise this time. Come back and we'll make a deal with you. If we give you the piece of Ly Erg's hand, you need to tell us where Gnogard is. No, you need to bring him to us. Then we'll make the exchange.'

A soot-covered ball of mist rocketed towards Brodie and stopped inches from his face. Charlie Boo uncurled himself and focused his eyes for two seconds to regain his balance before his eyes tumbled in opposite directions again. The young mist-spirit tumbled and turned, almost in time with his eyes – one way and then the other. He laughed and giggled continuously with not a care in the world.

'Gnogard. He's an old meanie, but I can try and find him for you.'

For once, McCloud seemed to be pleased with Charlie Boo. 'We don't usually negotiate, but it seems to be fair and reasonable. Charlie Boo – off you go and don't come back until he's found.' He then turned back to Brodie. 'And you – stay away from Gertruda. She's on to you Brodie. She's almost there – if you want to see home again and your family, stay away from her forest.'

'This is all your fault Brodie McHaggis.' Mildred looked at him matronly. 'If you hadn't come back to the Highlands, none of this would be happening. Ly Erg tried to stop you taking her back with you to wherever you came from, but you just humiliated him. Don't you see, he was doing you – and us – a favour.' Mildred flicked her eyes to McCloud nervously.

'We will be in touch,' said McCloud sternly, 'and in the meantime, I hope you like the jokes.' He laughed boldly and flew to one side. An ocean of misty eyes laughed back at them and the eagerly awaiting spirits started hurling their jokes at Brodie and Erin again.

'What's worse than finding a worm in your apple? Half a worm! Har, har, har, haaaaaar.'

'What did the traffic light say to the car? Turn around while I change. Aaggggghhhhhhaaaa, haaaaa, haaaaa.' Tears rolled down their faces and turned into icicles as the spirits churned their jokes out one after the other.

'Did ya hear aboot wee Jimmy?'

Brodie wasn't waiting around for anymore. His ears hurt. His brain thumped with the constant repeats of jokes so he spun on his heels and ran into the thick, dark forest.

'Brodie! Wait! Brodie!' Erin just caught sight of Brodie's ginger-red fur as he disappeared into the trees. She ran in after him.

It grew dark very quickly. Brodie stopped and waited for Erin. His chest wheezed like deflating bagpipes as he caught his breath.

'McCloud made us crash the truck to keep you away from Gertruda!' shouted Charlie Boo as he whooshed past Erin and Brodie, somersaulting backwards a number of times before getting dizzy and falling onto the ground where he lay giggling contentedly.

Erin and Brodie jumped around with fright. Before Charlie Boo could get another word out, a large ghostly hand grabbed the small mist-spirit by the shoulder and pulled him back out of the forest, weaving him through the trees. Charlie Boo just laughed and giggled as he bounced off a few trees on the way. 'Stay safe Brodie!' he chimed. 'See you later alligator, don't forget your toilet paper, ha, ha, ha!' His voice was like that of a ten-year old boy, only hollow.

Erin sighed heavily and looked down at Brodie. It was almost 3 o'clock and the short wintry afternoon was coming to an end. It would be dark very soon. They walked through the trees and left the forest further up to avoid the mist-spirits.

'They've gone.' Brodie peered into the mist cautiously. 'There's no noise. They've left us alone.'

Erin wasn't so sure. The mist had thinned out, but it was eerily quiet – too quiet in fact. There were no mist-spirits. No eyes looking at them from the mist. No jokes. No laughter and no terrible singing.

'Maybe they have gone. Right wee man, it's back into the rucksack for you.' She turned to pick Brodie up, but something had beaten her to it.

Brodie yelped. A sharp, stabbing pain seared through his shoulders as he was plucked from the ground like a daisy.

'Brodie! Brodie!' shouted Erin. 'Let him go, you freak!' Erin looked up at the large bird-like creature. It had short fat wings, the body of a lion and the beak of an albatross. It was Klutz. One of

Gertruda's soldiers. Brodie dangled helplessly from the creature's large claws as he soared into the mist. Erin looked about her. Dork was bound to be close by – she would be next.

CHAPTER TWELVE

Ginny-ging

Erin grew smaller as Brodie was lifted higher and higher from the ground. He floated into a giddy mist, unable to focus or take control of what was happening as anger raged through his body. His head swirled. He saw Noremac. No, he heard her voice. Just her voice. The next he was falling through the air.

Erin held out her arms and just managed to catch Brodie. She cradled him like a baby. Falling towards him was a large piece of heather, stained with his blood and weaved with the fur and feathers from Klutz. He smiled weakly. The Silent Protector had worked. He reached up to catch it when another bird-like creature swooped down from the trees, snapped up the heather and took off before Brodie could blink. The creature may have had the bulk of a lion, but he had the speed and swiftness of an eagle.

'That's Dork.' I knew he had to be around here somewhere. At least you got one of them. Are you hurt?' Erin asked cradling Brodie gently.

Pain seared through Brodie's shoulders as blood trickled from his wounds, matting his ginger-red fur. He tried to raise a smile, but the pain was too much.

Tears burned at Erin's eyes. 'I need to get you back inside. Be patient with me, Brodie.'

Brodie squeezed his eyes tight to shut out the pain as Erin eased him back into the rucksack. She carried it in her arms, barely daring to breath over it; worrying about how bad his injuries were.

'Are you happy now mist-spirits?! How about helping me to keep Brodie safe rather than dishing out curses.' Erin looked around. There was not a single mist-spirit to be seen. 'Typical. The first sign of trouble and the weasels run away. Well, we'll see about your stupid curse.'

'Don't underestimate our curse.' McCloud's voice boomed from within the mist. Erin couldn't see him, but he was watching her, just as he had promised.

'Tell Gnogard that we need his help. Tell him he owes me. Remind him about how I helped him when I was just four. Tell him or Gertruda will be joining you very soon!'

Erin's tearful shouts were met with a ghostly silence. She stepped around in a full circle, and then another, but not one mist-spirit showed itself. She and Brodie were alone. 'Cowards!'

Erin had managed to sneak back into her room unnoticed. Brodie watched quietly as she fussed over him, dabbing at his shoulders with white fluffy stuff. The fluffy stuff turned the water in the hand basin red with his blood. Erin grabbed another piece of cotton wool and continued to dab at his bloodied wounds.

Brodie flinched. It stung, but Erin's warm words and continuing chattering helped to sooth his pain. He sat with his three feet dangling in the hand basin in the grand bathroom as he listened to her plan how they were going to get him home. A now familiar feeling of deep sadness stabbed at his insides. Only, it felt worse every time it happened. A tear rolled from his eye and trickled down his funnelled nose, splashing into the red water.

'Why Brodie – you're crying.' Erin wiped the tears from his eyes, but each tear was replaced by another. Brodie reached for the one thing that made him happy. He began to sing.

The hairs on Erin's neck stood on end as the music sent chills through her body. She felt as though a thousand ants with frozen feet were running up and down her spine. It was hauntingly beautiful.

Brodie fanned his four nostrils at different times with his toe-like fingers. The music changed pitch and volume effortlessly, seamlessly. There were no words – just music. The sound of a few people playing the bagpipes, a long distance away, combined with a choir of the sweetest angels singing – almost like pan-bag-pipe music. So sweet, yet so haunting.

When Brodie finished, Erin's eyes were glistening with tears. She clapped her hands together in applause, but froze when she heard a muffled round of applause behind her. She swung around – but there was nothing there. Although she strangely felt the presence of a hundred pairs of ears.

Brodie hadn't noticed. His head remained bowed and his chest rose sharply and then fell slowly as he sighed deeply.

'That's so beautiful, Brodie.'

He tried to muster a smile. 'Thank you. So are you,' he said simply and hopped down from the basin. He stumbled badly as the pain shot through his shoulders. He was going nowhere fast.

Erin bent down and scooped Brodie up in her arms.

Brodie sighed again and felt his eyelids grow heavy. The pain eased as he drifted into a much-needed sleep after channelling his energies to turning Klutz into heather.

Erin's eyes filled with concern as she gently pushed Brodie under the bed. Her young face had taken on the responsibility of someone much older as she paced the room, fraught with ideas of how to get Brodie out of the Highlands and back to the safety of his home in Drumdrui.

'Coming down for dinner?'

Erin jolted nervously and swung her head over her right shoulder. Her mother had knocked on the door but she had been too deep in her own thoughts to hear anything. She rushed towards her mother to get her out of the room before Brodie started to snore.

'Yes, Mum. I'm absolutely starving. What are we having?'

Brenda smiled at her daughter to hide her concern. Erin looked so tired. And so worried for a ten-year old. She had to find out what was bothering her. As she pulled the door closed behind her, she noticed something odd in the corner of the room. Pausing briefly, she stepped back into the bedroom.

'Erin?'

Erin's stomach dropped to her knees and stayed there. She feared the worst and was just about to blurt out everything and ask her to help get Brodie home. Then she stopped. What if her mother couldn't see Brodie? Maybe HE was imaginary. Maybe SHE was going mad.

'What happened to these plants?' Brenda laughed loudly at the chewed plants standing in the far corner of the room. They looked like they had been attacked by a swarm of locusts for breakfast, lunch and dinner. Small slivers of leaf peppered the carpet around the plants.

Erin managed a smile and laughed. No wonder Brodie hadn't complained of hunger. She couldn't make out what the plants were supposed to have been, but Brodie had pretty much eaten all of them.

'I don't know Mum. They were like it when I came in. Strange, isn't it? Maybe it's some sort of topiary gone wrong? Wonder what shape they were trying to create?'

'How odd. I was sure they weren't like that earlier.' Brenda shrugged and laughed. She wrapped her arm around Erin's slim shoulders and ushered her out of the room. The air rushed from Erin's lungs as she let out a sigh of relief when the door clicked shut behind them.

The oddities didn't stop there. Goblins, heather-pixies and dozens of faeries of all different shapes, sizes and ugliness poured through the corridors and down the large staircase towards the dining room, chittering and chattering about what they were going to eat and take back with them as mementos.

'I tell you, I'm sleeping with the large diamond tonight. You can have it tomorrow night – or next year. I'm older and I need much more rejuvenation than you do.' An ugly faerie with bucked teeth, squint eyes and orange skin stomped down the stairs beside

Erin on two of her four stubby feet. Her friend, who was just as ugly but somewhat younger looking due to the absence of the folds of skin that her friend had, stomped off in front of her in defiance.

'Look, it's like this. It's survival of the fittest and I'll get there before you do. And I want my wings! To have wings is a dream come true. So tough luck on you, old wifie!' The young gallump stuck her orange tongue out, went down on all fours and rattled her bum cheeks at her before stomping off – at a quicker speed than the older gallump, but still not very fast in comparison to Erin. The old, creaky looking gallump moved at a snail's pace.

'I keep missing out,' she sighed dolefully, 'and the more I miss out, the older and weaker I get. I've been saving for this holiday for years … it's my last chance.' A large tear formed in her left eye as she struggled on, stomping and muttering to herself. 'I've missed it every night this week and I just don't have any energy left. If I don't get there tonight, then I'm not sure how much longer I can hang on to this old and frail body of mine. After all that I've done for those younger ones – mentored them, cared for them and supported them. And for what? To be kicked in the teeth for my kindness.' The gallump sobbed quietly to herself.

Erin felt a strong tug at her heart as the old, wrinkled faerie struggled to stomp her way down the stairs. Gallumps looked so awkward as they stomped everywhere. To have wings meant they could go wherever they wanted and a lot faster. Erin bent down and scooped the gallump up in her small hand.

'What have you got there, love?' asked her mother as she looked into the palm of her hand, but she couldn't see anything.

'Oh, I thought I saw something – but it seems that it was just a bit of dust.'

Brenda looked at her daughter and smiled warmly. 'Come – dinner is about to be served.'

Erin raised her forefinger to her closed mouth and winked at the gallump.

Ginny-ging stood on all fours on Erin's open hand and stared into Erin's large blue eyes. She looked down to the ground and when she saw that Erin had overtaken the younger, selfish gallump, she smiled gratefully at Erin through very old and tired eyes. The folds of orange skin around them draped like swag curtains and her teeth were cracked and stained brown.

Erin scanned the many faces in the bustling dining room looking for the young American lady wearing the diamond. She was already sitting down at the table. Erin threaded her way through the talkative people over to the table.

'Do you mind if I sit next to you?' Before the tanned lady could answer, Erin had already pulled out the chair and lowered herself onto it. She looked at the diamond as it sparkled brilliantly. Heather-pixies hovered around the woman's head, wanting to take an opportunity to swoop down onto the precious stone. Erin lifted her hand to the diamond. The gallump smiled widely through her wrinkled skin and she looked at the glistening stone, longingly.

'I hope you don't think me rude,' Erin began politely, 'but I just love your diamond. Can I touch it? I've never touched a real diamond before – or certainly not a diamond as large or expensive as this one.'

'Why of course you can,' the lady replied in a strong Californian accent. 'I keep this one in the safe at nights. Three million dollars it is worth,' she boasted pushing her neck forward with pride. 'I treated myself to it after I finished my last movie.'

Erin briefly touched the diamond. 'Wow – it feels wonderful.' The gallump raised her three-toed foot and also briefly touched the diamond. A spark and a faint glow of energy flowed from the diamond into the old gallump. To an untrained eye, the spark from the faerie just looked like light reflecting from the diamond. Nothing more.

Ginny-ging looked more energised already and she smiled back at Erin most gratefully. The lumpy, wrinkled skin on her back began to erupt as Erin looked on in horror. The gallump continued to smile, looking more energised as the seconds ticked by and two orange translucent wings emerged from her back.

'Thank you human one. I don't know why you have helped me, or why someone as old as you can even see me, but I now have my wings. I'll manage to get into the safe tonight to sleep with the diamond. Nobody else can claim it – it's mine for tonight. One night with it will give me many, many years of youth and many years with wings. I will be eternally grateful to you.'

Erin smiled at the gallump and thanked the lady for letting her examine the magnificent diamond. The younger gallump eventually stomped into the room and her face reddened as she saw what had taken place.

'There are some nice earrings here you can sleep with tonight,' said Ginny-ging triumphantly. 'It'll give you a few weeks – but not your wings. You're far too young for wings.' She smiled softly through eyes that showed many years of wisdom.

Erin hardly ate a thing, too engrossed in watching the hundreds of creatures running over the table, up the legs, down the curtains and swinging from the chandeliers. All unnoticed by the dinner guests. It was amazing – and fun. They were so careful not to disturb anything. To do that was a crime and they would be imprisoned for it, but the imps were more mischievous and played with the rules. They would tip over a glass of wine when someone's hand moved to pick up it up. Or when a glass of wine was set down on the table, they would tip it over so that the person thought he had done it himself. Whenever that happened, the impish giggles were so intense that it almost deafened Erin. It was the most entertaining evening that she had ever had.

After dinner, Erin burst back into the bedroom, her eyes as large as saucers. 'We're going home Brodie. The mist has gone and they've cleared the lorry away from the end of driveway. The road is now open.'

Brodie lifted his head and blinked sleepily at Erin's feet. He had been dreaming of home. He had just seen Iron McGillis getting yet another telling off from one of the oldest haggises, Hamish McTosh. What had seemed to be a strict and boring life at Drumdrui now seemed to be very appealing and pleasant to him. He sighed dolefully as Erin threw on her jacket and picked up her rucksack.

'Well, come on then. We're going home!'

Brodie looked at Erin with tired eyes. 'Can you take me back to the loch tonight?'

Erin shook her head. 'No silly. Gertruda will have it well guarded so you've no chance of getting away. We have to confront her and we have to find Gnogard. Come on,' she said shaking the bag at him to get in. Her ginger-red curls glowed with excitement against her pale skin.

Brodie stood up and stretched each of his legs one at a time, before limping over to Erin. His shoulders twinged as he twisted himself to get comfortable in the rucksack. Darkness closed in around him as Erin dropped the flap over Brodie and tied it securely before easing the bag over her shoulders.

Brodie could feel Erin's heart beating excitedly as he lay against her back. The bag swayed gently as Erin made her way down the large staircase, out of the front door and into the car. She stopped as many faeries, goblins and boglouts as she could and told them to put the word out that she was looking for Gnogard. 'He owes me one – remember to tell him that.' They looked at her horrified that she could actually see them and even more horrified that she was talking to them. Some of them tutted in disgust, and some stared in disbelief, wondering if they were imagining things.

The indicator ticked purposefully as Ralph pulled the car out of the drive and onto the main road, heading for home. Brodie was becoming used to the gentle hum of the engine and the swaying motion of the car – it didn't make him feel so queasy now. Erin leant her head back on the seat as she began planning their attack on Gertruda. Her thoughts were overtaken by the curse placed on them by McCloud – the Curse of the Scotch Mist. What did it all really mean for them?

CHAPTER THIRTEEN

Gnogard

The Scott's house remained shrouded in mist. Erin hummed thoughtfully and stroked her chin as her father steered the car up the driveway. The headlights lit up dozens of pairs of eyes peering over the rooftop at them, but for whatever reason, the mist-spirits didn't reveal themselves. They just remained a row of silent, blinking eyes.

The bright red front door of the house next door flew open and the yellow light from the hall shone like a torch into the misty night.

Rusty pushed past Rose's legs and bounded into the front garden to greet them, his tail flapping so hard that he almost took off. His slobbering tongue lashed around his mouth desperately looking for someone to lick. Rose tottered after him in her expensive, pink velvet slipperettes and grabbed him by the collar. Rusty sniffed the air and looked towards Erin. He let out a friendly bark and ran for the fence pulling Rose after him. Rose's heeled slipperettes dug into the ground as she was catapulted out of them and dragged across the lawn by Rusty.

Erin, Brenda and Ralph tried to conceal their smiles as Rose lifted her head from the muddy and grass-stained snow. Not able to contain himself anymore, Ralph dived into the house. 'Quick – inside. The dog's gone bananas! I've never seen him so friendly.'

Erin's heart somersaulted as William appeared in the doorway, his hands wedged in his jean pockets. She swooned at his perfect good looks, but his perfect nose was creased and his big brown eyes were reduced to narrow slits as he glared back at her. 'What have you done to our dog Erin? He's a beast. He's horrible! You've done something to turn him into a wimp!'

Erin's romantic visions of William were quickly shattered as she realised that he would never change. He would always be a bully.

Saliva bubbled and dripped from the dog's mouth as he continued to bark his way across the lawn towards them.

Erin and Brenda ran inside the house and Ralph slammed the door behind them laughing loudly. He stopped briefly to look out of the spyglass.

'I don't believe it. That darn dog is just sitting at our door, raising his front paw and whimpering like he has lost a friend and master.' The dog's large dark eyes looked up at Ralph dolefully. Then he saw Rose storming up the path after Rusty, which was enough to frighten grizzly bears into an early hibernation. 'You should see Rose's face!' Ralph placed his finger between his teeth to stop himself from laughing.

'That snow and mud will do her complexion wonders,' laughed Brenda, wiping the mascara-stained tears from her eyes.

'What about her designer labels … how will the stains come out of them?' Erin held her stomach as she laughed loudly. 'My sides hurt.'

Brodie laughed quietly – he found it extremely funny.

A loud banging sound interrupted the laughing and the house fell silent, apart from a few bursts of laughter trying to be contained by all of them.

Erin slipped up the stairs to her bedroom. She glanced back briefly when her father opened the door to see Rose covered in grass and snow. Her face was thunderous as her father tried to hide his laughs by coughing and clearing his throat. She heard her mother's muffled giggles as she hid behind the front door.

Safely enclosed in her own bedroom, Erin and Brodie laughed loudly at what had just happened. Brodie sounded like a winded bagpipe every time he laughed and Erin tried to quieten him down by getting him to laugh into her pillow. He had never had the occasion to laugh as much as this and he was enjoying it. Then he stopped, suddenly.

'What was that?' The tufts of ginger-red fur on the tips of Brodie's ears stood upright as he twitched them towards the window.

'What was what?' asked Erin. She wiped the tears of laughter from her eyes and walked across the room to the window. Pulling back the net curtain, she peered through the glass into the darkness, but all she could see was her own reflection and mist. 'It's too dark to see. Are you sure you heard something?'

Brodie nodded his head and then shook it. No. He wasn't sure.

Erin snapped the curtains shut and turned back to Brodie. 'Well, here's our plan of attack. I think we need to get some rest so that we can sneak out once Mum and Dad are asleep. By the sounds of it though, Rose Stewart is going to be with them all night complaining about what they have done to Rusty. Isn't it strange? He's just so friendly.'

Rose's annoying high-pitched wails drifted up from the kitchen below for some time. After setting the alarm on her mobile phone to wake her at midnight, Erin carefully placed the piece of red porcelain into a pocket on the side of the rucksack. She hung her clothes in the wardrobe and pulled on a pair of blue jeans and a black jumper.

'I'll just go to bed like this – saves me getting dressed again.' Erin pulled back the thick duvet and Brodie jumped in under it. She climbed in beside him, switched out the light and was asleep in seconds.

Brodie listened to her soft breathing for a while before he was engulfed by sleep. The white figure in the mist came towards him again, reaching out to touch him. He tried to move towards it, but his feet were stuck fast. He looked down at them, but as usual, they were surrounded by mist so he couldn't see what was holding him back.

'Believe in yourself Brodie,' whispered a sweet innocent

voice. 'Believe in yourself and believe in me.' The white figure moved closer to him and the mist began to clear, revealing the faint outline of a woman's face.

Just as before, Brodie didn't get the chance to see who was calling him from beyond the mist. A hideous cackling broke the peace and a black cloud began to smother the white figure. A screeching sound followed, like nails being dragged down a blackboard. Brodie tried to run towards the white figure – to help protect her, but an incredible force pulled at his feet.

His heart raced faster than he'd ever felt it race as he tried to protect his friend – or whoever belonged to the soothing voice. 'I believe in myself. I believe in myself. I'm doing like you told me to do. What good is it doing me now? I'm useless. I can't move. I can't do anything.' Everything was suddenly surrounded by darkness. All he could hear was a gentle tapping sound.

Then it stopped.

Brodie listened again.

There it was. Tap, tap, tap.

He opened his eyes widely. He'd been dreaming again. He was still in the bed next to Erin. She was sleeping comfortably.

Tap, tap, tap.

That wasn't a dream, that was real. Brodie slipped out of bed and onto the floor. His ears twitched as he listened closely, trying to locate where the sound was coming from.

Tap, tap, tap.

It was something at the window, but he hesitated before going to investigate. The last time he went to see what was at the window, he nearly fell to his death, was nearly eaten by next door's dog and was then unwittingly kidnapped by Gnogard. No, he wasn't going to fall for that again.

Tap, tap, tap.

Brodie paced the room.

Tap, tap, tap.

His inquisitive nature took over. He moved in behind the curtain and leapt up to the windowsill. All he could see was mist. Nothing else. No spirits, nothing.

'About time too!'

Brodie fell through the curtain and crashed to the floor, banging his head sharply. Feeling a bit dizzy, he regained his balance and ran back over to the bed to wake up Erin.

'Erin! Erin!' he shouted in a loud whisper, jumping up and down on the duvet frantically.

Erin felt the room shake and held onto the bed as though she was in an earthquake. She opened one eye first and then shut it.

'Erin! Hurry. It's Gnogard. He's outside!' Brodie wasn't going to let him in himself. The last time he saw Gnogard was at Urquhart Castle when he was with the goblins trying to take Gertruda back from them. She had promised to make him handsome, but Brodie had reduced him to a piece of green speckled heather which he and Erin had tossed into the bin with pleasure.

Erin threw back the duvet and lunged at the window.

'Hurry up – it's freezing out here.' Gnogard smiled widely at Erin and Brodie as he stood on the windowsill outside. He looked different. He was still as ugly as ever – so Gertruda hadn't given him the good looks that she had promised for turning Brodie over to her. His eyes were still almost on the sides of his head and his teeth were still as hideous as ever, but there was something behind his eyes and smile that was different.

Without hesitating, Erin opened the window carefully and pulled the gnome inside the bedroom. He was covered in droplets of mist.

'So, I hear you're looking for me?'

'How'd you get here so soon?' asked Brodie and Erin in unison.

'Ah well, news spreads quickly in my world. Anyway – great to see you Brodie.' He stretched out his grubby arms to embrace Brodie, but Brodie backed off.

'Awe – come on there pal. You did me a favour, you did. I have now felt what it's like to be a nice gnome and it's great. Erin – you were right back at Urquhart Castle. Since I've been nice, I've already got one dame interested in me – and that's just been in the last few hours. I may still be ugly, but she's seeing me in a different light. I've never had it so good,' he beamed revealing all of his teeth. He threw her a big friendly wink. 'I never want to go back to the way I was.'

'That's what Booger said!' Brodie looked at Erin sharply. 'And he got taken by Big Bag and Knobbly Knees. He's bound to be back under Gertruda's spell now.'

Gnogard's grin faded quickly and his eyes grew serious. 'Big Bag and Knobbly Knees you say?' He folded his arms and stroked his wrinkled chin. 'Well, that pair are bad news. If Gertruda's hired them, then she's promised them the earth. What does she want with that little snotbucket anyway? Thought she wanted rid of him?'

'I suspect that she didn't want him getting too close to us. You know, he was actually becoming a good friend.' Erin paused briefly and looked at Gnogard with sincerity. 'Can we begin to trust you in the same way? How do we know you're not working for that old witch?'

'Look, I can cross my heart and point to heaven that I'm not working for her. Brodie's my best pal now,' he chuckled throwing his arm around Brodie, who squirmed his way out of Gnogard's grip and quickly increased the gap between them.

'So, what do I owe you, Erin? I'm told that I owe you big time.'

Erin smiled memorably. 'Yes – remember those days when I kept you company and talked to you? Mum and Dad and the Stewarts next door thought that I was just talking to myself, but I was talking to you – remember? And I kept that scraggy mutt Rusty away from you too, or he'd still be peeing on you. I used to take you scraps of food and I used to read to you. I even took you inside one winter. I suppose you'll go back to your place in the garden now you're back?'

'Not on your life. I'm in danger of Gertruda turning me back into what I was – and I hate that. I'm starting my own life on the other side – and it's great. No more being a garden gnome. No more stealing, no more …'

'Anyway – back to what I need you to do for me,' said Erin with some urgency as she cut into Gnogard's speech. 'You don't disagree that you owe me – true?'

'Well … I suppose so ...'

'Good,' said Brodie as he interrupted the flow of conversation. 'Because you're gonna help us overthrow Gertruda.'

CHAPTER FOURTEEN

The Burning Hand

They had to wait nearly an hour before leaving the house to make sure that Mr and Mrs Scott were tucked up in their bed, fast asleep.

'Don't open it – the hinges will squeak and will wake everybody up,' Erin whispered as she climbed over the gate at the end of the garden. Brodie and Gnogard followed her. They looked back at the house, but it was already barely visible in the mist. They could hear Rusty barking next door at the Stewart's. Lights flicked on throughout the house.

'Hurry,' Erin whispered. 'Before they let that darn dog out.' They all ran towards the forest quickly and didn't stop until they were well away from the house. Brodie and Erin quickly told Gnogard about Ly Erg and the mist-spirits and the Curse of the Scotch Mist. Gnogard listened intently as he guided them through the thick mist towards the forest. He had an inbuilt radar that would take him anywhere, blindfolded. He scratched his matted hair and screwed up his dirt-engrained face as he looked at Erin.

'Doesn't look as though you've much choice but to give the piece of porcelain back to Ly Erg, I think.'

'What if he carries out his threat on Brodie?' Erin protested.

Gnogard shrugged his shoulders. 'Look at your options. Either you both live the rest of your lives with the Curse of the Scotch Mist, or you give Ly Erg his hand back and take the risk.' An evil grunt slipped through his dirt-engrained mouth, but then he straightened up and his face took on an air of sincerity. 'Why don't we just finish it now – that's what they want anyway. Get Brodie back home and stay away from Gertruda.'

'No, we must deal with Gertruda. I'm not even sure that I can get back home yet. I'll take the risk. I can't let Gertruda find the others – I *won't* let her,' Brodie said fiercely. He stared down at the hundreds of spiders' webs draped over the shrubs, heavy with droplets of mist. A large orange spider sat in wait in the middle of one of the webs. Without blinking, Gnogard snatched the spider from its web and rammed it into his mouth.

Brodie grimaced as he heard it crunch through Gnogard's stained teeth. Gnogard noticed Brodie's discomfort and grinned. A leg from the spider wriggled from the gap in the front of his teeth, but it disappeared as he crunched down on it again.

Brodie shuddered and followed Erin and the gnome as they scaled the large flagstone wall into the next field, chattering about old times when Erin used to go into the garden and keep him company. They were like friends reunited.

Erin stumbled over some clumps of snow-covered grass and landed on her knees. She laughed briefly before picking herself up and dusting the snow from her jeans.

'Brodie?'

Gnogard stopped laughing and looked around the ground as he detected the urgency in Erin's voice.

'Brodie,' she called again. 'Brodie! Where are you?' Erin's heart flipped.

Gnogard called for him too. 'Brodie, you little ginger-haired beastie – now's not the time to play hide and seek.'

Erin walked in circles in the mist. Gnogard followed her. Round and around and around in circles until even he lost his bearings.

'H-u-u-u-mph.'

'Brodie? Is that you? Where are you?' Erin yelled, peering through the mist.

The night air was silent as they waited for Brodie's voice again. Nothing. Until.

'H-u-u-u-mph.'

'Quick! This way,' said Gnogard hurriedly as he darted into

the mist. Erin followed him back to the flagstone wall and listened. It was silent. Apart from the sound of Erin's heart as it pushed the blood around her head fast, making her dizzy.

'H-u-u-u-mph.'

The noise came from behind the wall. Erin leant over it and jumped back with fright. Brodie stared back at her through a wide grin as one foot appeared over the wall, followed by another and then another. He pulled himself right up to the top of the wall and stood there looking so proud of himself. Thousands of droplets of water from the mist clung to his fur.

'And Mirg McVey says that haggises can't climb. Well – I've just proved that theory w-r-r-o-o-o-o-ng ...' Brodie lost his balance and tumbled head over heels into the snowy bracken below. He sounded like bagpipes being dropped from a great height as he screamed when he banged his nose on the ground and crushed one of his legs, sending pain shooting through his body. When Erin and Gnogard finally managed to dig him out of the bracken, he looked at them through tear-stained eyes. His nose throbbed painfully.

They looked back at the young haggis, trying not to laugh. Erin bent down and scooped Brodie in her arms through bouts of laughter. 'You poor wee beastie.' She gently kissed Brodie's nose and cradled him in her arms. He felt an immense warmth run through his body as she spoke softly to him.

When they arrived at the edge of the forest, Gnogard seemed hesitant. Fear flashed through his, normally, bold and brash eyes.

'What's wrong?' Erin looked at the gnome sternly. 'Remember – we're in this together.'

Gnogard shifted uncomfortably as he kicked at some icy snow on the ground and surveyed the opening to the forest. It was just visible through the mist. The fear continued to drip into his eyes and his stomach gurgled uncomfortably. Then his face changed as his wide mouth broke into an even wider smile, which disappeared around the sides of his face to where his eyes were. He coughed a nervous laugh and looked at Brodie.

'Ok you three-legged weirdo – let's go do it.'

'What do you mean weirdo? You're one to talk,' Brodie growled as he sprung from Erin's warm arms and tripled around the ground challenging him. 'Go on, explain yourself you ugly piece of work.'

Gnogard grinned even wider as Brodie growled like nothing he'd ever heard before. He laughed.

'I knew you couldn't change into something as nice as you claim to have. I just knew it. You're working for *her*, aren't you?'

The grin instantly disappeared from Gnogard's face and his eyes grew serious once again.

Erin sighed and placed her hands on her hips. 'Look you two – stop your bickering. Let's get a move on.'

'Not so fast, fearless one. You have something that I want.'

A long silence followed as they waited for something to appear from the mist. Then, eventually eyes appeared and McCloud and Mildred faded into view.

'Well, where is it?'

Brodie's fur bristled as he recognised the insignificant voice that had spoken to him the night before at the loch. Insignificant sounding he had thought, but obviously powerful. He stared into the dark eyes of the small soldier who walked out of the mist and stood in front of them. A faint light shone onto him from somewhere lighting him up in all his glory. He was dressed in a bright-red buttoned jacket. The red, gloved hand that he had used to threaten him with was tucked away in his pocket, out of sight.

Ly Erg stood no more than three feet high in the mist. He looked much like a wooden soldier from a Christmas decoration and just made you want to laugh at him. Only this time, Brodie didn't laugh. Nor did Erin. They just stared back at him in silence.

'Ah, not so brave this time, are we? That was a horrible,

disgusting, stinking thing that you did to me back at Loch Ness, Brodie. Particularly as I was only trying to help you – them,' the soldier said snootily as he looked around the mist-spirits. 'I really didn't deserve that.'

'You weren't trying to help Brodie – you were trying to help yourself,' spat Erin. 'You only wanted Gertruda … the heather … back so that you could be sure that she wouldn't succeed in her task and so that you and your mist-spirits wouldn't have to put up with her when she dies and joins you! You weren't trying to help Brodie at all. If you had been a bit more honest about your intentions, then maybe, just maybe, Brodie would have given you the heather.'

Ly Erg's eyes turned red and shone brightly onto Erin. She glowed red and felt something run through her – something hot – something warning her off.

'You, young girl are too big for your own boots. Now – give me back the piece of my hand or suffer the Curse of the Scotch Mist.'

'Why is it so important that you get it back?' demanded Brodie, coming to Erin's defence. Ly Erg changed his reddened stare to Brodie and he too felt the dangerous warmth flow through his body. He backed off.

'I need it to survive … that's all.' He hesitated. 'Just like you need your lungs to breath ... that's it, I need it to survive.'

'If I give it back to you – will you reverse the threat that you put on Brodie?'

The soldier's thin mouth smiled widely, but his eyes didn't match the amount of smile that he gave. There was something lacking in them. 'Why, of course I will.' He moved his gaze to Brodie and continued to smile.

'How can we be sure?' asked Gnogard scratching at his chin wistfully with his bitten, dirt stained nails. He had, until now, remained in the background, listening. He stepped forward and faced the fragile looking soldier. Gnogard was much shorter than him, but he could have knocked the soldier over by just blowing on him.

Ly Erg's smile faltered for a second and then widened even more if that was possible. 'Why my dear old Gnogard. You will just have to take my word for it then, won't you? My word is my word.'

Brodie started dancing around Ly Erg, back and forth like a guard dog with three legs, staring him out, sniffing the air around him and growling softly. He couldn't be sure whether to trust him. Why, he could just knock him out right now with his powerful smell and they could take the rest of his hand when he turned to porcelain and broke into a thousand pieces.

'No Brodie – I wouldn't do that again if I were you. Not a good idea at all.' Ly Erg's smile faded until his mouth returned to a thin straight line. 'Now, my hand?' Ly Erg removed his hand from his pocket and pushed it in front of Erin. It was no longer red. It was like a burnt smouldering piece of charcoal, with a hole in the middle the size of the missing piece of porcelain. He looked to be in pain as he stretched it out towards her.

'You took it Erin – so you must replace it,' he said firmly.

Erin pinched her nose with her fingers. The smell was disgusting – like burning flesh.

Brodie's stomach churned and he felt sick.

'You can see why I want my hand back, can't you?' Ly Erg whimpered, trying to get sympathy from Erin. 'I have been in constant pain, and I cannot help my friends here if I don't have the use of my hand.'

Hundreds of eyes appeared in the mist and then bodies formed around them. They were completely surround by mist-spirits. The air remained still and quiet.

McCloud swooped in just above Ly Erg's head and spoke directly to Erin.

'If you refuse to help, remember, the Curse of the Scotch Mist will be with you forever. You can never escape it.'

'Oh haggiswallop,' snapped Brodie as he kicked at the misty air. 'Lies, lies and more lies.'

McCloud narrowed his eyes, but the red eye in the middle widened and glowed even brighter. The lines on his forehead crinkled into deep crevices as he leant down towards Brodie.

'Now listen here young haggis. If Gertruda joins us, it means that she's killed all of the haggises. Then she will take over our world and cause total misery to us. Our only escape is to live in this world – permanently. It's not great. In fact, we hate it, but living with Gertruda would be worse. So, my hairy little beastie – if your friend here doesn't obey, then she'll be seeing a lot more of us. We'll be there when she wakes up in the morning, even in her dreams. We will never let her forget the misery that you will have brought to us.'

Erin began to shudder as she felt the cold seep through her bones. She couldn't live a life like that. She had to do something, but she didn't trust Ly Erg. If she gave Ly Erg's hand back, then the solider would have the chance to kill Brodie. If she didn't, then Gertruda would have the chance to kill not only Brodie, but all of the haggises and she would be cursed for life. She was torn in two.

'Just say we hand it back to you,' said Gnogard wryly. 'What's to say that you don't harm Brodie?'

The worms on Mildred's brows wriggled angrily and the scars on her face bulged as if something was trying to get out. She folded her arms strongly and stuck her upturned nose into the air. 'You will just have to trust him,' she said dryly.

Gnogard wasn't happy with her response. 'How will you stop Gertruda achieving her vow? Will you let Brodie go home when you get your hand back?'

Brodie tripled around the mist-spirits, looking at their different shapes, sizes and weirdness. They were very wary of him and some disappeared in a pop, only to reappear when Brodie had moved away from them.

'Er … yes … er … I give you my word,' said Ly Erg moving steadily closer to Erin. He pushed his upturned hand under her nose. Erin retched.

The mist-spirits sounded like wind howling around the eaves of a house as they echoed Ly Erg. 'I give you my word.'

Brodie looked to Erin.

Erin looked to Gnogard.

Gnogard shrugged his shoulders and raised his thick eyebrows. 'You heard the man – he gives you his word. What more can you ask for? Any faerie of his stature that gives you his word means it.'

Erin swallowed slowly through her dry throat and set the rucksack on the ground. She took off her gloves, unzipped the pocket on the side of the rucksack and reached inside to retrieve the porcelain.

Brodie's heart pounded as Erin stretched her arm forward and displayed the bright red porcelain against the white skin on her palm. Excitement flooded his body at the thought of being free – of going home soon. Images of his home flashed in front of him. Images of his mother nursing young haggisen in The Bothy. Of his father at Darmaeddie Loch as he asked questions about the kelpie and the witches. He so longed to be back at home in the warmth and security that he was in only days ago. How so much had changed in such a short time.

Ly Erg's eyes widened with relief. 'You must replace it,' he instructed in a slightly quivering voice.

Erin obeyed and picked the porcelain from her hand, lowering it over the soldier's blackened hand. The porcelain glowed an intense red as she moved closer to the hole in Ly Erg's hand. She hesitated and studied his puny features.

'What are you waiting for? Get on with it, lass!'

Erin took a deep breath and lowered it to his hand.

Brodie and Gnogard watched with abated breath.

The mist-spirits crowded around and watched too. The air was silent. Ly Erg smiled smugly – his powers would soon be returned. It would all soon be over.

CHAPTER FIFTEEN

Brodie's Dilemma

'You moth-ridden old bag – I told you we'd taken the wrong turning. Can't see a darn thing in this mist.'

'You thieving old elf. I told you we should've gone back that way!'

Brodie instantly recognised the voices. Big Bag and Knobbly Knees.

THWACK!

The skinny, sly-looking elf appeared out of the mist and bumped into Erin and Ly Erg.

'Er – sorry there … can't find my way in this mist,' he apologised, taking off his pointed cap and placing it across his chest as he bowed politely. His head was thinly covered with hair, revealing a splattering of freckles on his scalp.

'Told you – you never listen to me you ugly old brute!' Big Bag appeared out of the mist on the other side of Erin and Ly Erg, who both stood gobsmacked at the two quarrelling creatures.

'Look, if you don't stop arguing with me, I'll trade you in for a new model – old bag!' Hatred flashed through his eyes as Knobbly Knees glared at the large old carpetbag.

Big Bag simply shrugged him off like he had done for decades. 'Well go ahead and do it. Then at least I can retire and maybe begin to have a good life instead of being chained to a cruel master like you.' The bag's large eyes drooped momentarily, then they picked up slightly as he arched his bushy eyebrows. 'But I know that you can't do without me. I've been your right arm for longer than you can remember. What would you do without my guidance – eh?' A glint flashed through his eyes as he dared the elf to sack him.

'Do you really think that I'd let you off the hook so soon? You've done a really bad job so far and I'm not finished with you yet. You've got a lot to learn, so, heel, Big Bag. We've got places to go, people to see and things to … er …' he looked around him and noticed that all of the mist-spirits, Ly Erg, Erin, Brodie and Gnogard were watching them intently. '… er and things to see,' he repeated. His voice clinked like a rattling chain.

'Tell the truth for once and shame the devil. You mean things to steal, you old crook!' snapped the bag as the two of them drifted off into the mist. Their arguing and bickering finally faded out until there was nothing left but a stunned silence. After a few moments, Ly Erg spoke up.

'Strange. Very strange,' he muttered as he turned his head back to Erin. 'Now, where were we? Oh yes,' he said looking down at his black, smouldering hand as small wisps of smoke puffed from it. 'You were going to replace my piece of hand.' A slow cruel twist entered his face as he stared intensely at Erin.

Erin's hand had remained in the same position above Ly Erg's hand throughout the bizarre scene with Big Bag and Knobbly Knees. She released the grip between her thumb and forefinger to let the piece of porcelain drop into the soldier's hand, but nothing dropped. There was nothing there but fresh air. Erin felt faint and could barely speak.

'But … I don't understand … what happened to it?'

The red veins in Ly Erg's eyes pulsed so strongly they almost burst.

Brodie and Gnogard stood aghast.

After a few silent moments, everyone scrabbled around the icy wet ground looking for it. The mist-spirits flew around in a frenzy looking under every frozen piece of grass, but it wasn't there.

McCloud dropped in front of Erin's face and challenged her. His large body shimmered with mist. 'Where is it, Erin? We won't put up with your tricks and games. You will be cursed, so don't mess with us – do you hear?'

Brodie stood in front of Erin and bared his crooked, yellow teeth. 'She's not lying. She doesn't know!' He jumped and flicked at the ground with his feet like an angry dog as he defended his young friend.

Erin bent down and picked him up. He continued to growl and his legs scrabbled around in the air as though he was cycling.

'He's right – I don't know where it is. I must've dropped it so you'll just have to keep looking. Now, if you don't mind, I have a haggis to save,' said Erin politely but firmly. Without hesitation, she turned to head towards the forest, but the mist had become so thick, she had no idea which way to go.

Gnogard raised his hand to her. 'Erin – don't mess with them. They are very serious, and you will get hurt.'

Erin stared helplessly into the gnome's wide eyes. She didn't know what to do.

Gnogard stepped aside and stood face to face with Ly Erg.

Ly Erg tried to look into the gnome's eyes, but he found himself looking into one eye, then moving his gaze across his wide face to look into the other eye.

The young mist-spirit, Charlie Boo, swooped down from the sky. He turned somersaults and bumped into one spirit after the other. They grabbed at the air trying to catch him, but Charlie Boo was too full of energy and kept dodging their attempts. He whizzed around the mist and pulled up in front of Brodie. His eyes stopped spinning for just a few moments whilst he looked at Brodie. They were tinged with sadness.

'You've got to get out of here. Go to the forest and fight Gertruda.'

'Will you get that stupid good for nothing joker out of here!' shouted Ly Erg. 'I thought you had already taken care of him.'

'I thought I had too,' McCloud yelled, 'but the little imbecile keeps coming back!'

'Brodie, Brodie, Brodie. Ly Erg has tricked you. He's too scared and too weak to fight Gertruda. The only way he can stop her achieving her vow is to kill you with his threat before you leave here. Go to the forest now – he can't get you in there. Go. NOW!' The yellow spirit began to giggle and splutter again as if it was all a joke, but there was a note of urgency in his young voice.

Brodie ran from side to side and around and around as he wondered which way to go. Every hair on his body stood on end and an intense cold shivered through his bones.

'Quick – this way,' shouted Gnogard. 'QUICKLY! If they find that piece of hand Brodie, you're done for – now move those three legs as fast as you have ever done in your life!'

Erin scooped Brodie up in her arms and ran after Gnogard.

The mist-spirits surrounded them trying to make their visibility as poor as possible. Even Gnogard started to doubt the way to the forest as his gnome homing device was hugely interfered with. He ran around in circles and sniffed at the air, trying to decide where they were and which way they had to go.

Erin's heart banged hard as she screamed at the mist-spirits diving her from every angle and hurling joke after joke after joke at her.

'Why did the sand cry, Erin? Because the seaweed, har, har, har.'

'What do you get if you cross a duck with a firework, Erin? A firequacker! Hee, hee, hee, har, har.'

'Doctor, Doctor. How do I stop my nose from running? Stick your foot out and trip it up, Erin!'

'What is evil and ugly on the inside and green on the outside, Erin? A witch dressed as a cucumber!'

'You mean Gertruda dressed as a cucumber,' quipped another mist-spirit.

'Har, har, hee, hee – maybe I doooo.'

'What is wrong with twin witches, Erin? You won't know

which witch is which!'

Mildred dropped from the sky into Erin's path. 'This is what your life will be like forever if Ly Erg can't have Brodie. Let him go you foolish girl.'

Erin gritted her teeth hard and pushed her way through the spirits. She felt like she was being stabbed with ice picks. She was cold and drained, but she pushed on through.

Brodie heard something familiar. He screamed at the top of his voice, like a bagpipe in a lot of pain. The mist-spirits backed off immediately and the jokes stopped.

'Do you hear it Erin? The sound of rustling leaves in the treetops. The dryads! Quick – follow the leaves!'

'What?' Gnogard looked at Brodie very confused.

'Just follow the sound of the leaves. We'll be safe.'

'Keep screaming Brodie – the mist-spirits don't like it.'

They stumbled through the mist and made their way towards the sound of the leaves. The trees came into view so abruptly that Gnogard almost smacked into one. Once inside the belt of rowan trees, the mist had cleared, but the sound of rustling leaves was almost deafening.

'I don't understand,' Gnogard quizzed, scratching his head as he looked around the bare treetops. There wasn't a leaf in sight. Or any wind.

Erin and Brodie craned their necks and looked up at the trees. 'Dryads,' said Brodie through a large smile. He felt safe. For now.

'Dry what?' asked Gnogard picking at the flaking skin around his bulbous nose.

'Dryads,' Brodie repeated. 'Look hard into the treetops – you'll see them soon.'

Gnogard craned his neck. Sure enough, one by one the dryads appeared out of the trunks and branches of their trees. They were translucent at first. He began to see dozens of young nymph-like faeries climbing around their trees. They had green tinged hair, almost translucent wings, and skin the same colour and texture as the bark on the trees. Their ears were like the knots in the trees, and their faces were long and pointed. They stared down at them.

'Why haven't I ever seen them before?' asked Gnogard quizzically as he admired the delicate creatures. They stared back at him from their warm brown eyes.

'We love air, so we stay up here,' said one of the dryads in a melodic, friendly voice. 'We hardly ever reveal ourselves ... but Brodie is in danger.' She turned her gaze to Brodie.

'Hello again Brodie.' The dryad looked a lot stronger than the last time that she had seen the haggis. She had drained all of her energy saving Erin just short ago.

'Hello … dryad.'

'Berina. Call me Berina. Brodie – why have you come back? You were in terrible danger the last time we spoke. You're in even more danger now and I'm not sure if we can help you this time. Gertruda has strengthened her army and she's made sure that you can't use the Silent Protector on any of them.'

Brodie sucked in a sharp breath and held it for a few seconds before exhaling strongly through puffed cheeks. His long nose fluttered and his nostrils quivered nervously. He turned to Erin.

'Erin?'

Erin looked at the fear in Brodie's eyes. She was beginning to fear for herself as well. She had been well and truly sucked into the other world and they would do to her what was necessary – human or not. She shook her head slowly and tears welled in her eyes.

Brodie turned to Gnogard.

'Well, don't look at me you ginger-red pain in the backside. My life was hassle-free until you came along.'

'Gnogard! Just remember – you owe us. If it wasn't for Brodie, you'd still be miserable and you wouldn't have got a chance to experience the good side of life.'

Gnogard glared back at Erin. She was right, but he didn't know what to do just as much as Brodie and Erin didn't know what to do.

A twig cracked in the forest behind them and they all swung around to see who it was. They saw nobody.

The leafless trees rustled as though a strong wind had begun to blow. 'Please, you must go and sort out your troubles – we cannot become involved.' Berina began to fade back into her tree. 'You must believe in yourself and you must fight for your life. We can only protect you here because Gertruda will not come near us for fear of us draining her energy. She can only leave the forest on invitation by a human. Once you leave our forest, we cannot protect you.'

The other dryads also began to fade back into their trees. As they did, they repeated Berina's final words. 'We cannot protect you …' Their voices willowed gently through the forest until they had completely disappeared and all that remained was the sound of leaves rustling gently.

'We need to find Gertruda and settle this once and for all.' Gnogard stood firm.

Brodie felt faint. His legs went weak. 'I could stay in this forest for the rest of my life – I'd be safe.' He sounded unsure.

'Not much of a forest though,' said Gnogard surveying the narrow strip of trees that lined one side of Gertruda's forest.

Brodie nodded in agreement. He looked behind him. 'If I go back the way, then I have to face Ly Erg.' A shudder worked its way quickly down his spine and through each of his leathery legs as he tripled around the rowan trees thinking through his dilemma.

'And if I go in there, then Gertruda will have me for sure – and the rest of the haggis community.' He paused and looked up at the trees. Erin and Gnogard waited silently. Brodie finally made a decision.

'It's only a matter of time before either of them gets

someone in here to flush me out. So, it's not safe to stay here and it will only bring danger to others. I have to go out there into the mist. I have to sacrifice myself for my own stupidity and save the haggis community from being destroyed by Gertruda.' Brodie's eyes deepened and large black rings formed under them. He sighed miserably and began to head back towards the mist.

The trees began to rustle violently, as if to warn Brodie. He peered up to the treetops in search of the dryads, but they remained invisible.

He changed his direction and began to walk towards the fir trees and the rustle of leaves and the swaying of the trees died down.

Erin looked at Brodie and then craned her neck up to the tree where Berina lived. 'So, you're saying he should confront Gertruda?'

The ground beneath them quivered slightly and the bracken rustled, but nothing appeared. The forest fell silent.

Brodie decided what he was going to do and continued his way into the dark forest. Erin followed and as she passed by Gnogard, she jabbed him in the shoulder. 'You're coming too,' she instructed. 'He needs all the help he can get.'

CHAPTER SIXTEEN

Inside Gertruda's Cottage

Gnogard reluctantly turned on his heel and followed them into the forest. It grew darker and colder. The peaty ground crackled loudly after each step they took and turned to solid ice. Pausing for a brief moment, they looked behind them. Everything they had walked through had turned to ice. Large icicles were hanging from the trees; birds and insects were frozen to the spot and their breath turned to ice and dropped to the ground like hailstones.

An icy chill ran through Brodie's twenty-four toes, up along his legs and into his spine. The icy air chaffed his nose and icicles had formed on his fur, hanging from his brows like ice curtains. Small icicles formed on the delicate hairs on Erin's face and she shivered uncontrollably. Her hair was frozen solid and would snap at the slightest touch. Even Gnogard was being severely challenged by the unusual penetrating cold, despite the many snowy nights he had spent outdoors in the garden.

They eventually reached the familiar snowless glade. Gertruda's glade. It was dimly lit. It looked warm and inviting. So warm that Brodie just kept walking straight up to the front of Gertruda's broken down stone cottage. It was surrounded by a meadow of juicy, purple thistles just waiting to be eaten. Brodie's stomach grumbled. A warm, orange glow oozed from the windows and the doorway of the cottage. Warm, orange smoke bellowed out of the crumbling chimney and orange glowing lights shone in the sky above it. The ice immediately melted away from Brodie's fur, replaced by an incredible inner warmth.

Erin followed Brodie – mesmerised by the inviting cottage. A cottage that she had never seen before in the forest until a few days ago. A cottage that had seemed so cold, dingy and uninviting then, now seemed more appealing to her than the gingerbread house did to Hansel and Gretel. She followed Brodie as he walked to the doorway, his teeth chattering less as his body warmed up.

Gnogard followed them.

An intense warmth flowed up through their bones and into their blood as they stepped inside the cottage, making them feel woozy and very, very comfortable. The large portrait of Alexander McHaggerty, almost a storey high, greeted them, lit up by gargoyle candleholders at each side. The flicker from the flames brought Alexander's eyes to life. He was a hard looking man with a large, very prominent nose. There wasn't a line on his face. He was young. Erin wondered how Gertruda could ever have been attracted to such a hard and cruel-looking man.

Gertruda blamed the haggis for her loved one, Alexander McHaggerty, discovering that she was the spawn of a black witch. When Alexander had entered the forbidden forest to hunt the haggis – he had stumbled across Gertruda's cottage – her mother's cottage at the time. She had never told him who she really was and he had, by accident and by his greed to find the haggis, found her there caring for her old mother. He had ruthlessly cast her aside, just in the same way as her father had cast aside her mother. Until then, Gertruda had remained a good witch. She had begged Alexander not to reject her – that she wasn't a witch, but he had refused. She had transformed into a black witch right in front of his very eyes. Gertruda had never stopped loving Alexander, who died shortly after with all of his family in a mysterious house fire.

The only way the spell could be removed from the McNorris family was for three generations of witches to live a life of harmony, without losing their temper, but none had. When each McNorris transformed into a black witch, she had to remain in the forest for the rest of her life, unless invited out by humans. Most died after a couple of hundred years of black magic and torturing those around them. Gertruda had vowed not to die until every last haggis was dead – but she didn't reckon on it being so difficult.

Gertruda hadn't reckoned on the white witch, Noremac, helping the haggis to escape to the peaceful village of Drumdrui. Noremac had blessed them with the power to turn enemies into friends after briefly turning them into lucky white heather. Noremac was no longer around and Gertruda was unpicking her spell, bit by bit. She was so close to achieving her vow. So close.

Brodie scanned his eyes around the inside of the cottage. It was more spacious than it looked from the outside. A large worm-ridden table sat at one side of the only room inside the cottage, and four rickety worm-eaten chairs were neatly tucked in underneath it. Some spiders rested in their webs around the corners of the room and others scuttled across the dark ceiling, busy spinning more webs. Gnogard licked his lips as his attention moved to the spiders.

A bright orange fire roared in the hearth under a very well used black kettle hanging from a large hook. Steam was puffing out of the spout, waiting for somebody to lift the kettle from the hook and pour hot berry juice into the four empty cups on the table, but there was nobody there.

Brodie scanned the room for Kittikens – Gertruda's large black panther. There was no sign of him either. It was just so peaceful. He looked at Erin and Gnogard. They had the same look of warmth about them, ready to collapse into one of the rickety chairs and drink hot berry juice.

The door suddenly slammed shut behind them and a harsh cackle penetrated their ears. Brodie held two of his three feet over his ears to stop the pain and he hopped on the other. Erin and Gnogard cupped their hands over their ears, but the cackle penetrated their hands and vibrated their brains so hard that they soon snapped out of their warm orange trance.

It seemed like an eternity before the cackling stopped. Brodie rushed to the door, but it wouldn't open. There was no handle on it. He clawed at the edges. Erin tried as well until her fingers bled, but the door wouldn't move.

Erin ran to the window and peered through the cobweb-covered glass. Dork and Klutz were lying lazily in front of the cottage – in their own way guarding it.

'We're trapped!' Brodie whined. 'Trapped again – how did she fool us?'

'Don't beat yourself up about it,' said Gnogard earnestly. She had us all fooled – she used some tranquillising potion to get us in here – why else would we be standing in this flea pit?'

Brodie looked around the cottage again. It had lost its warm cosiness that had drawn them into it. It suddenly looked murky, old and threatening. He shuddered as a large fat spider with five legs scuttled by his feet. Gnogard chased it into the corner.

'Can't you do something, Brodie?'

Brodie looked helplessly at Erin. 'Like what? Turn the cottage into heather? Turn the door into heather? I don't think so.'

Erin patted Brodie on the head gently to say that she understood. They were trapped.

The darkened room began to flicker from a bright orange glow in the far corner, opposite the door. All three of them turned and crept cautiously towards the glow. They stood at the top of a stone spiral staircase, which seemed to lead down into the depths of the earth.

'What do you reckon?' asked Erin.

'There is no way I'm going down there,' scoffed Gnogard as he took one step back.

'Well – what else can we do? Break the window and get out of here?' Erin stood challengingly with her hands on her hips, then stormed across the room, grabbed one of the worm-eaten chairs and launched it at the window, but it just crumbled into sawdust. She beat on the glass with her bare fists, but it didn't even vibrate.

'There is only one way out ...' Gertruda's gravelly voice drifted up the stairs into the room. Faint black smoke drifted from the stairway and as Gertruda spoke, the smoke formed a wispy black mouth and mimed her words.

'The only way out Brodie, is to give me what I want.'

A pain stabbed at Brodie's stomach as Gertruda made her demands. He became very angry. It was working. His anger would force the Silent Protector to help him. He smiled and puffed out his small, furry chest as he moved towards the smoking lips. 'All I need to do is turn that old witch back into heather.'

'Wait Brodie – you can't go down there!' shouted Erin.

'She's right, young haggis. If you go down there – it's the last we'll see of you.'

Brodie wasn't listening now. He was in a trance, ready to defend himself against his enemy. He walked to the stairs. The mouth vanished in a puff of smoke. Brodie began to descend the stone stairs. Reluctantly, Erin followed him and descended each stair with caution. Small burning torches dimly lit the stairs. They spiralled down, down, down into the depths of the earth, eventually opening out into a large underground cave. The air was very moist and humid. A large black cauldron, steaming over an open fire in the middle of the cave provided the only means of light.

Brodie ran his eyes around the dimly lit cave. He couldn't see Gertruda, but he could hear her raspy breathing close by. After a few minutes, a black, cloaked figure emerged from the shadows. Another cloaked figure emerged from the other side of the cave and they both walked slowly towards them.

Brodie looked from cloak to cloak. His heart beat faster the closer they got to him. His throat ran dry. Which witch was which?

Skeletal, wart-covered hands fell from the second cloaked figure. It had to be Gertruda. Brodie tripled over to her and tugged at the dusty, dirt engrained cloak with his teeth until the hood fell down, revealing the witch's grey, wart-covered face. The hairs on the end of each wart wiggled like fingers trying to grasp at Brodie. Gertruda smelt like rotting flesh.

Brodie looked at the other cloaked figure.

Erin followed his gaze – who could it be?

'Well, well my dears. Back again – sorry you had to leave so quickly the last time – without a party, ha, ha, ha …' Gertruda cackled for some minutes before composing herself. She turned her black eyes on Brodie and stared long and hard at him.

Brodie began to fade in and out of consciousness as his anger rose again.

'No need to try that one Brodie McHaggis. You can't turn any of us into your precious friendly, lucky white heather. Euch! How could Noremac be so cruel as to turn enemies into friends! Well, it didn't work on me, thankfully.' A child-like smile spread across the witch's bony face as she dropped her head to one side and stroked the quivering wart on the end of her pointed chin.

Brodie was well under his own hypnotic spell trying to use the Silent Protector. After a few minutes, he collapsed from exhaustion.

'Brodie! Brodie!' Erin shouted desperately.

Brodie felt very drained, but a smile crossed his face. 'We're free to go now, but we'll have to hurry – Gertruda doesn't last long under the spell.' Brodie noticed the fear in Erin's eyes. 'What's wrong?'

Erin looked away from him.

Brodie looked towards the boiling cauldron.

'Not this time Brodie. Ha, ha, ha. I worked out the code, remember? And all I needed was some of your blood to reverse the spell on the others. You can't put any of us under now.'

'But … how …' Brodie sprang to his feet and took a few steps back as he squared up and faced the haggard old witch.

She smiled openly at him before her face turned thunderous. 'Remember Dork and Klutz back at your fancy Skibo Castle? Well, it was all Booger's idea – he didn't stay your friend for long – not after I broke the spell.'

The moss-covered ghillie dhu stepped out from behind the cauldron and glared at Brodie. He began to outstretch his arms to encircle them around Brodie.

'Careful now you little snotbucket – remember. You can't have Brodie. Erin's yours for the taking. Brodie's mine.' Gertruda laughed insanely. 'As if he could ever have been your friend anyway. Utter poppycock!'

Of course. Brodie remembered how Klutz had gripped him hard with his sharp claws and pierced his skin, making him bleed. When he had turned the bird-like creature into heather, Dork had swept down and taken the heather back to Gertruda, speckled with his blood. He eyed the ghillie dhu with spite. He knew that he couldn't trust something that had been so evil. Gertruda had managed to win him back too easily. He had been duped.

'So, Brodie. By that sudden realisation on your face, I don't need to tell you how I did it? Clever old dear, aren't I?' Her icy cackle echoed around the cave and shook Brodie's bones. There was no escape from Gertruda now. Nobody would stop her – especially not a young, insignificant haggis like him. He had triple-handedly endangered the haggis to extinction. His mother's eyes flashed in front of him. His father's stern voice echoed in his head instructing him to stay away from the loch and to forget all of the nonsense about the myths and legends because they didn't exist. Had his father known what he would find? Had he known about Gertruda all along? The cave began to vibrate and swirl. Brodie felt the ground rush up to meet him as he passed out.

CHAPTER SEVENTEEN

A Bad Omen

Hundreds of boglouts and goblins now filled the cave, ready to witness whatever Gertruda had planned for Brodie and Erin. The noise of their chatter became deafening as they giggled and sniggered boglishly with one another, their brown beady eyes penetrating poor Brodie as he lay on the ground unconscious. Erin was stooped over his limp body, trying to wake him up.

Silence filled the air and all eyes turned to the cauldron from where green and red smoke bellowed upwards, smothering the cave roof. The ghillie dhu stood beside it like a dutiful soldier.

'Come now Kittikens – come see our visitors,' said Gertruda in a child-like voice. 'They didn't stay long the last time – I know you're very upset with that, aren't you my wee kitty? You didn't get to play with them.' Gertruda cackled loudly.

The ghillie dhu beckoned to the sleek black panther as it emerged from behind the cauldron. The diamond-studded collar sparkled brilliantly through the green and red smoke, and displayed a kaleidoscope of colours onto the uneven walls. Kittiken's eyes shone like black pearls and his teeth flashed like tusks of ivory.

'He thinks that you don't like him because you ran away from him the last time. Not so this time, eh?' The panther's tail flicked wildly as he stood beside Gertruda and purred loudly.

Erin panicked about home and how long she had been gone. She looked at her watch. Just like the last time, it had stopped at the moment she had entered the forest. So how long had she been here? Was it any time at all? What time was it in the faerie world? Did time even exist with them?

Brodie stirred. He coughed the dryness from his throat and looked up at Erin. His eyes widened. 'Erin! Behind you!'

The other cloaked figure moved forward from the shadows and whispered something into Gertruda's shrivelled, dried up ear. She cackled heartily, dried the tears from her menacing eyes and then returned her cold gaze to Brodie.

'Well, my wee haggis – you've decided to join us again have you? Why don't you tell me all about yourself and your family. I am so looking forward to it,' she laughed insanely, 'and then, you can take me back with you to meet them properly this time. Now, isn't that nice? Booger – heel!' She pointed to the ground by her feet and the ghillie dhu obeyed her immediately.

Brodie's anger snapped. He jumped to his feet, stomped up to Gertruda and looked fiercely into her eyes, then he shot a glare at the ghillie dhu. He had never known what it was to hate, but he could only imagine that the feeling he had now was one of pure hatred. It hurt. He raged inside.

'Never! Never, ever, ever you rotten old witch. You won't get my family,' he said snarling and spitting at her.

A strong, male hand emerged from the other black cloak and pressed firmly on Brodie's head as he tried to head-butt Gertruda. His feet kept sliding over the dusty cave floor as he continued to run hard at the witch, but he couldn't get beyond the strong hand.

Erin ran over to the cloaked figure and yanked the hood down. She gasped loudly and took a few steps backwards, never taking her eyes from the person beneath the hood. Her blood chilled.

'Why it's … y … you?' Erin felt uneasy as she stared at the man in disbelief.

'Yes, it's me.' A cruel smile played around the man's unshaven face and his eyes twinkled with malice.

'You were at the loch too? Watching us? I thought I saw something. The cloak – your cloak. I tripped on it, didn't I … ?'

'Smart girl. I was at the loch and saw Brodie reduce Ly Erg to a pile of broken porcelain. Funniest thing I've seen in years. Shame he couldn't get that part of his hand back,' he said slyly as a deep chuckle played around in the base of his throat. 'Booger – have you got it locked up safely?'

The ghillie dhu nodded obediently.

'Yes, another great idea from Booger. I believe that Ly Erg is still looking for it out there in the mist.' Fergus Munro threw his head back in laughter. 'Thanks to Big Bag and Knobbly Knees, yet again.'

Everything slotted into place now. Erin recalled how Knobbly Knees had bumped into her and Ly Erg in the mist. The porcelain must've dropped from her fingers into the bag's mouth. Of course. She looked at Fergus Munro. He had posed as the taxi driver who had driven them to and from Urquhart Castle just the other night. He had tried to frighten her about the Scotch Mist and all along, he had been right. No wonder he could see through the mist. He wasn't human at all – he was one of them.

'No, I'm not one of them,' he said as if he had read Erin's thoughts, but he could read her questioning eyes quite clearly.

'So who are you then?' asked Brodie as he stopped trying to head-butt Gertruda and looked up at the cloaked man.

'Gertruda's great, great, great nephew, of course,' he grinned. 'I'm Fergus Munro'.

Brodie was becoming more confused.

Erin wasn't. 'So you didn't lie about your name – at least that's something. I take it your mother is the one who is getting anger management classes then? So that she can rid your family of this curse? So you can all be white witches? You're on the third and last generation to break the curse – is that correct?'

The man nodded encouragingly and grinned slyly.

'And you want to help your great, great … great aunty to die so that she can go on to live a peaceful life with the mist-spirits? In the hope that she will be reunited with Alexander McHaggerty?'

He nodded again. 'Quite a bright girl, aren't we?'

'And you would be happy to see Brodie and all of his family

murdered just because of that spiteful old witch there. You would see the end of a species just because of her?'

He grinned again. 'Look – let's not get personal here. It's just business. She needs my help. And besides, nobody would miss the haggis. After all, the haggis is only a myth.'

Brodie growled fiercely and bared his teeth at the cloaked man.

'What's in it for you? What happens if you get angry? Does the same thing happen to you as it did to Gertruda? Or is the curse just on the McNorris women?'

Fergus Munro's eyebrow's knitted together in a puzzled expression as he tried to fathom out where Erin's questions were leading. 'Possibly. I'm not sure,' he said hesitantly. He looked confused as Erin continued to hurl the questions at him.

'Enough, enough,' Gertruda cried, becoming irritated with the sensible conversation. She wanted to get back to causing her usual havoc and mayhem. Erin ignored the witch.

'How many men are in your family?'

'I'm the first in generations.'

'Oh, well, try this for size you ugly old spawn of a witch. How angry will this make you?' Erin kicked her foot hard into Fergus's shin. When he jumped up and down cradling his leg, she kicked higher into his groin and he fell to the ground in an agonising heap.

'Now run Brodie!' Erin turned for the stairs. Brodie ran with her as they scaled them, side-by-side. The stairs seemed endless as they coiled around and around and around. Brodie was exhausted. How much further? It was like every step he scaled, another one was added. Footsteps echoed below as they were followed up the staircase by Gertruda, Fergus Munro and by the sounds of it, an army of boglouts.

'We're nearly there,' Erin said trying to sound encouraging through puffs of winded breath, but she didn't know what to do once they got to the top. They were still trapped, and with an angrier bunch of faeries and witches behind them. They fell up the last few steps and threw themselves into the room of the cottage.

'Gnogard! They're coming! Quick!' Erin looked around but Gnogard was nowhere to be seen, apart from a large pile of peaty soil in the middle of the cottage where he had dug his way out.

'I new that slimy gnome couldn't be trusted. He's tricked us into coming in here. He's so selfish – wanting his good looks all along. Imagine – I fell for his charm that he didn't want to be good looking as he had found love. What a liar!'

Brodie hadn't seen Erin go so red in the face before. Her hair glowed like it was on fire. She turned and looked at him with helplessness in her eyes. 'I'm sorry little one. I really am. There's nothing else I can do – I don't know how either of us will ever get away from Gertruda this time …'

Brodie just stared blankly back at Erin. All of the commotion happening around them faded away as he looked into her young, tear-stained eyes. They were helpless. He felt a somewhat strange, floating feeling as everything around him grew darker and darker.

Gertruda's voice continued to echo from the stairs below and Fergus Munro's footsteps grew louder.

Erin scanned the room swiftly looking for an escape, but there was no way out. Not even down Gnogard's escape tunnel because as a gnome burrows, he backfills the hole.

Fergus was almost at the top of the stairs.

The front door of the cottage suddenly burst open and a strong gust of wind brushed Brodie's fur straight back against his body. He looked nervously at Erin as they stood looking out into the snowless glade.

Gertruda and Fergus Munro appeared at the top of the stairs with dozens of boglouts and goblins surrounding them, foaming at the mouth and ready to sink their teeth into Brodie.

Gertruda raised her skeletal, wart-covered hand towards the door and her bony forefinger glowed red. Just as she was about to magic the door shut, her arm slumped to her side and she backed off into the corner of the room, cowering in the shadows. Her eyes continued to glow red and her breath rattled sharply.

'Fergus – get rid of them. Fergus! Do something!' Gertruda sounded scared.

'Do what, Aunty?'

Gertruda was now very weak, but she managed to raise her hand to point towards the door. 'Get rid of THEM,' she spat as she continued to shrink into the shadows.

Fergus, Erin and Brodie looked back towards the door. One, small orange gallump was hovering in the doorway. Nothing else. Just one small, insignificant gallump.

'Hi Erin!' Ginny-ging flapped around outside the door looking refreshed and so much younger than when Erin and seen her at Skibo Castle. The gallump's wings beat hard as she hovered in front of her, smiling through a row of crooked and uneven teeth. All of the lines in her orange skin seemed to have been ironed flat and her eyes sparkled with youth.

'Ginny-ging! What are you doing here? You are supposed to be at the castle, sleeping with your diamond.'

Ginny-ging smiled widely. 'Your friends said that you were in trouble and … well, one good turn deserves another. Besides, I've got someone looking after the diamond for me until I return.'

Brodie stepped forward and surveyed the funny creature as she continued to hover in front of Erin's face.

'Who are these friends?' he asked.

'You've got so many friends, young Brodie, but there is no time to explain – we must get you out of here.'

Erin and Brodie exchanged confused glances.

'We don't understand – what can you do for us?'

'You must move quickly. A strong gallump with her wings

entering a witch's house is a bad omen for her. I haven't entered it yet, but if she doesn't let you go, I will. She won't dare use her magic on a winged gallump. Go, now. I have only one chance to do this – I cannot re-enter the forest after this. I will stay here until you are clear of the forest. After that, you have Ly Erg to deal with. I'm sorry, but I can't help you there.'

A lump formed in Brodie's throat as he stared at the ugly gallump. He felt an overwhelming sense of guilt at even thinking that she looked ugly, especially as she was putting her own life in danger to save his life. His flute-shaped nose quivered as he began to sob uncontrollably. He just couldn't stop. The kindness was too much for him. He felt a sudden sharp pain around his ears as Erin slapped him.

'For goodness sake Brodie! Stop being a girl and let's get the heck out of here – NOW! After you – now run as fast as you can back to the edge of the forest.'

As soon as Brodie stepped outside of the cottage, the peaty forest floor quivered and vibrated and hard-faced, venom-spitting boglouts broke their way through the surface. Their brown eyes and fangs glinted at Brodie as they dared him to move one step further.

Brodie turned to the left, then to the right, but they were all around the glade. There was no way through the foot high wall of boglouts. Their sharp fangs would rip through his fur without much encouragement.

A bright light shone from above as Gertruda's voice bounced around the glade. 'Let them go … let them go … if this little runt of a gallump enters my house, I may never have the good fortune to achieve my vow and kill every haggis there is. So, let them go … for now …' Gertruda's voice trailed off into a long and sharp cackle that tingled every spine in the forest. Even the trees seemed to shiver as her voice travelled through their trunks.

Brodie looked at the boglouts' peaty-brown faces sneering back at him. He moved forward one step. The boglouts moved forward one step and leaned towards him, hissing and taunting him. He edged his way closer and closer to them, his heart banging hard against his chest as their pointed, meaningful fangs glistened challengingly at him.

Erin moved forward with Brodie. 'You heard what the old witch said – move it buster!' She kicked one very sturdy boglout out of the way and he rocketed through the air, but there was another one behind him to take his place.

Brodie reversed off, crouched down on his haunches, and lunged at the boglout, head-butting him out of the way. The boglout rolled over in the peat and the others hissed again at Brodie and Erin. Another boglout stepped in front of him, followed by another ten. There was no way through them.

A red beam of light flashed through the forest and blew some of the boglouts up into the air.

'I said LET THEM GOOOOO!!!'

The remaining several hundred boglouts hissed and spat at Erin but refused to break their wall.

Brodie raised his head high and walked straight into the boglouts and only when he was one millimetre from them did they begin to part and allow an exit through them. He wore a triumphant look on his face as he tripled through the ten-feet thick wall of seething boglouts. Erin followed at his side, continually wary of how close some of their teeth got to her legs.

Brodie felt a familiar rumble in his bowel as he neared the edge of the glade. An evil smile crossed his face and a glint of mischief flashed through his crystal-blue eyes. 'On three – run,' he whispered, 'and don't breath in for at least ten long seconds.' He winked at Erin.

Erin knew immediately what was next and she pulled her jacket up around her mouth and nose.

Brodie's bowel rumbled excitedly and burst loudly into the army of boglouts. When Erin looked back, most of them had passed out on the forest floor whilst others staggered around like drunken peats. Not that she would normally condone such behaviour, but she couldn't help but raise a smile.

'Brodie – you little imp.' She chuckled as they swiftly made their way through the dark forest and passed by tree, after tree, after tree.

'It's not getting any lighter in here. It's getting darker and the forest is thickening.' Brodie stepped around in a circle, but he couldn't decide which way to go.

Erin tried looking through the trees ahead, but it was like searching for a black cat in a dark room. Their pathway had disappeared.

'What's that noise?'

'What noise?' asked Brodie as a wash of fear ran down his spine.

'Listen … that noise. Like knocking.'

Brodie trembled even more.

'There. It's louder now – and faster.' Erin looked down and rolled her eyes – Brodie's three knees were knocking together.

'It's you – you furry haggis. Pull yourself together. We have to get out of this fir-lined jungle and you've got to be strong.'

Brodie straightened himself up and tried to be strong, but his legs just wobbled under his weight as he followed Erin through the forest into complete blackness.

After ten minutes of blind walking, the trees cleared to reveal a small, very dark and boggy swamp. They crouched behind some trees and looked across the swamp at the outline of a figure. Long, spiky pines stuck out of the folds of skin on the back of his neck. His saggy, wrinkled skin was covered in patches of brown hair. There was almost something goat-like about his head and legs, as if an old man was trying to emerge from a goat's body.

The creature turned his head slowly towards them, blood trickling from the corners of his mouth as he ate his way through a small carcass. His bulbous eyes blinked slowly in his large misshapen head. The urisk looked saddened and embarrassed.

'I'm sorry Brodie – but you weren't meant to see that. This is how I live, and I'm not proud of it. It's lonely and depressing here. I see nobody and nobody normally sees me. I live on the swamp's vermin.' He threw the remainder of the carcass into the swamp and it gurgled down into the thick, murky water.

Erin jerked back at the grotesque sight of the urisk, but she began to warm to him as she made contact with his compassionate eyes. She remembered how he had helped to save her life. How he had carried her through the forest, even though she was larger than him, until he had reached the dryads and begged them to save her. She owed so much to him – and the dryads.

'What brings you back into the forest – especially here? It's no place for anyone.'

Erin watched the hedgehog pines on the back of the urisk's neck move like fingers as he spoke gently to them. The compassion in his eyes once again concealed his hideousness. He was such a genuine creature that Erin wanted to wrap her arms around him and absorb his pain, but she couldn't bring herself to do it. He noticed her hesitation.

'Please – I want to be your friends. Can I help?' The urisk waded through the swamp and stepped out onto dry ground. Slimy, peaty water dripped from his hideous skin.

Brodie took a step back and shuddered.

The urisk stepped back behind a tree realising that he was causing a disturbance. His eyes saddened.

Erin hesitated, but then walked towards the tortured creature and raised her hand to his shoulder. The urisk's face filled with energy and warmth as Erin touched him. A smile formed around his wrinkled mouth.

'Yes – we would love for you to help us … again. We already can't thank you enough and we are embarrassed at having to ask you again.' She related to him what had just happened back at the glade. She spoke with haste.

'We need to get out of here – quickly – and we need to avoid the Scotch Mist.'

'They tricked you into coming this way. Not even Gertruda will visit this part of the forest. She was probably hoping to send in some of her cronies to find you later on – after Ginny-ging had flown off. Stay close and I will take you out the secret way, but it won't be pleasant.' His swampy voice trailed off.

Brodie looked at Erin for approval and they both nodded at the urisk. What could be more unpleasant than what they had just witnessed? Only, it was. They walked through forest that was so dark, damp and smelly that Brodie was nearly sick. Erin didn't understand how she had never seen any of this before. She thought her father had walked her through the entire forest.

Spiders, the size of dinner plates, sat in their oversized webs, waiting for their lunch to visit them. One black spider with red and green spots was watching a typically strange creature as it sucked at the sap on one of the tree trunks – much like a preying mantis who had lived his life on cheeseburgers, fizzy drink and sweets.

When the spider pounced on the creature, Brodie closed his eyes tightly, but he heard the crunches of the bones as the spider snared the creature and crushed it with its large hairy legs. He dared not look back.

'Can't we go any faster?' he groaned.

'I promise you – this way is quicker and safer for you.'

Brodie saw something else at the corner of his eye. He didn't care to stay around to find out what size of body belonged to the red eyes staring at him. He tucked in closely at Erin's heels as they trudged through the damp and sticky forest.

Most of the tree trunks were deformed. A strange, gluey substance leaked from them like tears of pain. The whole atmosphere of the forest was sad. Unwanted. Forgotten.

'Almost there,' said the urisk in a warm voice, which just didn't match his appearance or that part of the forest. No wonder he welcomed visitors and friends.

The forest began to lighten as the trees thinned and some moonlight eventually broke through. It shone onto something on the forest floor, making it sparkle red and green.

'Oooh – look at that beautiful stone,' cooed Brodie. 'I've never seen anything so pretty.'

Erin bent down and picked up a strawberry sized red and green jewel. It sparkled brightly and reflected on her face. 'It's so beautiful. I wonder who could've lost this. It looks … expensive. Obviously taken from Skibo Castle by some of the faeries.' She held it up to the moon and the ground became dappled with red and green light. Sighing thoughtfully, she put it into her pocket. She would get it back to its rightful owners somehow.

The urisk signalled to Erin to bend towards him. Erin lowered her head and he pressed his grotesque mouth into her ear. Erin's eyes widened with shock as he whispered to her, then she smiled gratefully at the urisk.

'Thank you, once again.'

'You must go now, and this is where I must say goodbye. It's dangerous for me out there. Take care little haggis … remember to visit me Erin – just contact me through the dryads … '

'Dangerous – but why …?' Before Brodie could finish his sentence, the urisk was swallowed up by the dark dampness of the forest. He was gone.

Erin reached into her pocket, wrapped her hand tightly around the jewel, and pulled it out. Turning into the dark forest, she threw the jewel with all the strength that she could find. There was a loud scream – Gertruda's scream – as the jewel slammed into a tree and fell to the ground.

'Not this time Gertruda McNorris. We're not taking you out of the forest a second time you old witch!' Erin picked up Brodie and ran as fast as she could into the rowan trees before Gertruda emerged from the jewel. Back to safety, she set Brodie down and he tripled his way through the trees beside her as they made their way back to the edge of the forest.

A large thumping noise began to vibrate the forest around them. Brodie began to see double vision, then triple vision, as the vibrations grew stronger and stronger.

'Quick – keep moving!' Erin shouted. 'Whatever it is, it's coming our way. Run!'

CHAPTER EIGHTEEN

Basher McSporran

'When will I ever be able to stop running?' Brodie wailed, keeping close to Erin's heels as they darted through the forest.

'Right here, right now.' A broad, husky Highland voice bellowed from the darkness.

Brodie was drawn back by the voice and he stopped and turned around. He wheezed like droning bagpipes as he caught his breath.

Erin stopped too and caught her breath.

They both peered into the darkness. Something whooshed past Brodie's four nostrils and beat down on the ground so hard in front of him that his brain vibrated and made his vision blurred again. He screeched loudly. A three feet tall silhouette stood in front of him, its purple eyes peering out of the dark forest. They blinked – twice. Then the voice spoke again.

'I said you can stop running – right here, right now.' The eyes surveyed Brodie carefully. 'And it seems that you have. Good.' A row of pearly white teeth smiled back at Brodie as the silhouette guffawed.

There was a sound of a match being struck, followed by a dim glow from a lantern, bringing the silhouette to life with colour and presence to reveal another weird creation of the faerie world.

'Well, well. It's been a long time since we saw a haggis around these parts.' The creature's black skin was tinged with green stripes going in different directions. The green differed in shades and looked suspiciously like black-watch tartan.

Erin smiled in disbelief at the colour of his skin. She had always thought tartan was something made up by the Scottish – not copied from an actual living being. Then, she was in the faerie world, so who was to say that anything was real. When the creature's club-shaped fist whooshed past her face and hit the ground like a ten tonne bullet, she brought herself back to the moment.

'What's tae smile aboot?' the purple-eyed creature asked as he studied Erin with intrigue. 'Hmmmm, I've never been this close to a human being before,' he said, parting his beetroot-red lips into a wide, almost charming grin. 'Pretty one too,' he muttered before turning his attention back to Brodie. His thick, wide nose was pierced with two thin sharp pieces of grey slate. Four inches of purple hair stood erect on top of his round head as his hardened purple eyes burned into Brodie.

Brodie's stomach rumbled with hunger as the creature reminded him of a thistle. He noticed the very strong and very powerful shoulders just two inches above the creature's waist. Two strong arms hung from them, one resembling a large club. He traced his eyes along the tartan-shaded skin. It sagged around the creature's bulbous hips and flapped like a kilt around its wrinkly knees. The absence of a neck and a waist made its two legs look ultra long. It had two long middle toes and two short crooked toes on each foot with curly nails that were shedding like flaky peat.

The sound of more matches being struck was followed by dozens of small lanterns lighting up around the forest, revealing an angry tribe of the strange creatures flanking their leader. They were slightly smaller, but very similar, apart from their eyes and mouths. Some had bulbous eyes, some were small and beady, and some were long and wide. Their mouths seemed to match whatever shape their eyes were, but despite their weird formation, they had the most charming of smiles. Their pure white teeth sparkled so brightly that Brodie became hypnotised by them. The leader raised his clubbed arm above Brodie, clenched his fist tightly and brought it down hard above his head.

'Brodie!' Erin just managed to push Brodie out of the way and the back of her shoe took most of the force. She screamed loudly and Brodie woke from his hypnotic state.

'What are they, Erin?'

'No idea!' shouted Erin as she ran to Brodie's side.

'No idea! No idea! No idea!' the creatures all chanted.

The leader stepped forward.

'The name's McSporran. Basher McSporran.' He raised his hands to his hips and stood with his elbows pointing outwards. 'But you can call me McSporran to save any confusion.'

'Because my name's Basher too.'

'And so's mine.'

'I'm Basher too.'

'And so am I. Basher McNicol.'

'And I'm Basher McGrory.'

The sentence was echoed again and again as each of the creatures stepped forward and identified himself as another Basher.

McSporran turned to face the other Bashers and they all became silent. He turned back to Brodie and Erin. 'And tonight, we'd like to be called Haggis-bashers!'

Every Basher laughed loudly and slapped their thighs at the apparent joke. Their laughter was so infectious that Erin and Brodie joined in until they were laughing so hard, they forgot about the danger surrounding them.

'We can crush a haggis in one blow,' McSporran bellowed, lifting his clubbed arm. The muscles rippled under the faint, tartan-shaded skin as he taunted them in front of Brodie. 'No haggis has ever been known to escape these arms. Word's out that there's a bounty on your head Brodie. So – either you come with us or you're mincemeat.'

'You mean haggis meat,' said a voice from behind him.

Erin managed to stop laughing and snatched Brodie in her arms.

'Yeah, but have you ever outrun a human?' She poked her tongue out at them, turned on her heel and started to wind her way through the trees towards the moonlight. Her feet became tangled in something and she felt the full force of the forest floor slam into her face as she tripped.

Brodie was catapulted through the air and landed high up in the branches of a rowan tree. He looked down and saw Erin lying on the ground calling for him, but she was safer if he remained in hiding. Until he could think of what to do. His heart pounded furiously. His head swam with anger as he watched the Bashers circle Erin. She was defenceless.

They thumped the ground around her demanding to know where Brodie was. Erin lay speechless as the circle of haggis-bashers closed in on her.

Brodie felt a familiar feeling rush through him as he drifted in and out of consciousness until he blacked out just as he fell from the tree.

CHAPTER NINETEEN

Harold Gunn

White mist swirled around Brodie as he tried to move. Like so many times before, his feet were stuck fast and he couldn't see what was holding them – all he could see was mist.

Noremac's pale face drifted in and out of the mist as she urged him to be strong – not angry. An icy gust of wind blew into his eyes and momentarily, the mist cleared. Brodie's heart melted at the beautiful image in front of him. The most beautiful face he had ever seen. The woman was wrapped in a white cloak. The hood fell around her porcelain-white face and her brunette hair tumbled down to her neck. Her smooth pink lips parted gently as she smiled at him and raised a pale hand of support.

'Brodie – be strong, young haggis. Think of those that you love. Be strong.' The face was quickly covered my mist again as the icy wind blew. The familiar scratching of nails down a blackboard echoed as the black mist began to smother the white mist. Brodie's breath was being sucked away. He clawed at his throat as he shouted for Noremac.

'It's ok, Brodie. I'm here. I'm here.' Erin looked down into Brodie's ginger-red face. Her read hair poked out from under her hat. Her face was just as white as Noremac's and her blue eyes were full of warmth. The same warmth that he first saw just days ago when she found him washed up on the shores of Loch Ness.

Brodie groaned. 'My head hurts.'

'No wonder you bag of troublesome fur. You fell head first from the tree. I'm sure you'll survive. Now, look what you did this time. Seems like it wasn't Gertruda they were working for.'

Brodie rolled over and stood on his feet as he looked around at the dozens of pieces of lucky white heather, each with a neat black-watch tartan bow tied around it.

'You mean …?'

'Yes Brodie. You did this. Hopefully they won't be calling themselves haggis-bashers when they wake up – unless Gertruda gets a hold of them.'

'She's used all of her antidote. The only way she can make more is to get more haggis blood.'

Brodie smiled at the familiar voice of the dryad and craned his neck as he looked up into the bare tops of the rowan trees.

'Did you push me out of the tree then?' he asked jokingly.

The bark moved slightly and the nymph-like dryad emerged from the tree and sat on the branch above them.

'Well Brodie McHaggis, I never! If it wasn't for me, you would have fallen the first time. I caught you.'

Brodie smiled teasingly. 'Thank you Berina.'

The dryad's eyes grew troubled and she tilted her head towards the sky.

'Go now, but tread carefully. There are many rivers to cross – don't test the depth with both feet. So long … maybe you can sing for us again another time.'

The familiar rustle of leaves echoed around the forest and the dryad merged back into the tree. Brodie could see her eyes blink and then they disappeared. Small flashes dotted around the trees as the other dryads blinked their eyes, until they too disappeared.

'What did she mean?' asked Brodie as he tripled around the tree trying to make sense of her mumblings.

'Simple Brodie. If you test the depth of the river with both feet – you will fall in if it's too deep. Then you might drown. That's exactly why you're in this danger now.'

Brodie's eyes crossed over as his brain fuzzed. 'I didn't see any rivers …'

Erin laughed. 'No silly – she's just saying that you jump before you think. Slow down, be logical and think a bit about what you're doing before you jump. Look before you leap.'

Brodie nodded his head slowly and when Erin turned away from him he screwed up his nose and mouthed her words. 'Bossy females,' he muttered.

Erin smiled and walked towards the edge of the forest. The mist was still very thick, but there didn't seem to be any mist-spirits around.

'Right – we need to be quick. Stay close.' Erin edged into the mist.

Brodie followed her. Then his air and light was snuffed out, plunging him into complete darkness as a sack drew down over him. He felt himself being hauled into the air.

'Ow! Erin? Erin! Help me, Erin!' Brodie kept screaming. He was jostled around as whoever had him began to run.

Erin turned back. 'Brodie?' She screamed loudly as she caught sight of a large figure running past her in the mist. She grabbed at the mysterious figure but she missed. Then she saw a glint of gold. It was Harold Gunn's gold tooth!

'Give him back you horrible man. You can't have him. He's not going to end up on your table!'

The butcher turned away and his large frame burst through the mist as he ran from Erin. His large bottom jumped up and down and his four chins flapped about like jelly as he ran awkwardly.

Erin quickly lost sight of him, but she could hear his breath rasp sharply against his chest. She heard another voice.

'Veer left. Veer right. Continue for one hundred yards.'

Harold Gunn stopped just as the flagstone wall came into view. He had made it over once tonight, and he would have to make it back. He leant over the wall and set the sack with Brodie in on the ground. He then heaved himself up on the wall and rolled over it on his belly.

'Continue for fifty yards.'

'Ok, ok you silly woman. I'm going as fast as I can!'

Harold wheezed as he rolled over the wall. He took the small satellite navigation machine out of his pocket and looked at the map to see where he had to go. He had programmed it to take him straight back to his van because he knew that he wouldn't be able to see through the mist. And he knew he had to make a quick getaway.

'Continue for fifty yards,' it repeated again. Harold tutted and stuffed the machine back into his pocket.

All Brodie could see was blackness. He could only hear voices. Mr Gunn's voice was one of them. He had been waiting for the opportunity to turn him into heather – now had to be the right time!

'Mr Gunn! Mr Gunn! Bring back Brodie! MR GUNN!'

Erin hurdled the wall like it wasn't there and ran up behind the butcher, kicking him hard in the back of his knee. His leg buckled under his weight and he crashed to the ground in pain. Erin stared down at the man as he rolled himself upright and stared back at her, beads of sweat running down his bright red face.

'You shouldn't have done that, Erin. Trust me. I'm on your side. You have to believe me when I say we've got very little time to get Brodie back to the loch. I'm trying to help him!'

Erin's jaw dropped open.

CHAPTER TWENTY

Return to Loch Ness

Erin stood opened mouthed as she watched Harold Gunn struggle to get himself up from the ground. He extended a hand to her for assistance as the satellite navigation voice spoke again.

'Veer left and continue for fifty yards.'

'Look, Erin. Just stay calm and keep close. I'll explain later. What we have to concentrate on is getting this haggis back to where he belongs …' The butcher hesitated. His usually sparkly eyes were full of concern. 'Ly Erg will stop at nothing.'

Erin blinked in astonishment. How did he know any of that? How could he?

'Trust me Erin – I know what's been going on. We have to move fast. Brodie has to get back to Drumdrui tonight.'

Erin had no option than to trust the butcher. She held out her hand and helped pull him back to his feet. She untied the rope around the neck of the bag to see Brodie. He was in a trance.

'Oh no!' She shook Brodie hard. 'Brodie – no. Not Mr Gunn. He's here to help us. Don't do it Brodie!'

'Do what?' asked the butcher.

Erin looked at the man, panic spread all over her face. Soon he would be lucky white heather. Only it wouldn't be lucky for them because he seemed to be their only hope in getting back to the loch.

Brodie finally opened his eyes and growled when he caught sight of Harold. This was his chance and Erin was ruining it.

'He's here to help, Brodie. We have to trust him. Don't do anything to him.' She sighed, relieved that she had just stopped him from casting his spell. 'Can't we take Brodie to the loch behind my house?' she asked turning back to Harold Gunn.

'No – it's too shallow, and too far away for Nessie. We need to get back to Urquhart Castle – and quickly.' Droplets of sweat continued to run from his red face as he breathed heavily.

'Yes – quickly. Quickly, quickly, QUICKLY! Get him out of here. Quickly!'

Erin and Harold jumped back from one another as Charlie Boo forced his bright yellow face between them. He laughed and laughed and chattered as his eyes rolled in opposite directions.

'They are coming to get you. Go now. Go NOW!' he pleaded. Then he was gone.

'Proceed forty yards to your destination.'

'Not far now,' said Harold as they stumbled over lumps of sodden grass and pockets of snow.

Brodie was cold, tired and hungry. 'It's ok Brodie,' Erin whispered to him through the sack from time to time. 'You'll be home soon.'

'And you'll soon be cursed by the Scotch Mist, Erin Scott.'

Erin and Harold were stopped in their tacks as the mist grew so thick, even the satellite navigation became confused.

McCloud's blue-tinged body moved across their path. His fangs glistened. His voice was definite and the red eye in the middle of his forehead continued to pulse like an angry heart.

Hundreds of other mist-spirits gathered around them, but they remained quiet. No jokes were said. No talking. Just an eerie silence.

Ly Erg emerged from the mist like an important celebrity, a smug smile playing around his boyish face. His cheeks glowed red and he puffed his chest up before extending his charcoaled hand to Erin. A strong pungent smell drifted up Erin's nostrils and she jerked her head back, shooting a fiery glare at Ly Erg.

'I tell you – I don't have it. Go and ask Gertruda for it and leave us be!'

'You took it, so you have to return it – soon. Your time is running out, young lady.'

A purple streak circled Erin and Ly Erg a few times before it emerged as Mildred. Swishing in beside the small soldier, she folded her arms and stared pointedly at Erin. The worms on her brow looked as angry as she did and mist escaped through the scars on her face like a steaming kettle. 'You must get it back – soon.'

'Look. Go and find Big Bag and Knobbly Knees. I'm sure they can steal it back for you. They stole it from me. Negotiate with them – NOT ME!' Erin stamped her foot hard.

Ly Erg, McCloud, Mildred and all of the mist-spirits shook their heads and silently pointed to Erin.

'You have arrived at your destination.' The satellite navigation burst into life again. Harold looked around. The van must be right beside them. It must be, but where? He grabbed Erin's arm and led her through the mist-spirits. Icicles stabbed at his skin and sent a shallow coldness through his bones, but Harold wasn't going to let them get in their way.

'Find a place to U-turn and proceed to your destination.'

He was going the wrong way. He gripped Erin's arm tighter and turned around. They could see nothing but mist. Erin's arm hurt.

'Over there!' Erin flinched as his grip tightened even more around her arm. The faint yellow glow of the van's headlights became brighter as they ran towards it. Harold Gunn hauled the door open and pushed Erin into the passenger seat. He slammed the door shut, then ran around to the driver's door, hauled it open and flung himself into the seat. The van shook violently under his weight. He fumbled to get the key in the ignition, started the engine and then spent a few moments fiddling with the satellite navigation machine to set a new destination point. Urquhart Castle.

'There's no mist at the castle just now. If we can get out of this mist quickly, we should be able to make it to the castle before it catches up with us. Only thing is, once we're out of the mist, Gertruda will be able to put us back on her radar. So, we've got to be slick. It's full steam ahead!'

The butcher managed half a smile as he placed the black box onto a holder on the dashboard, slammed his door shut and drove as quickly as he could through the mist. The road in front of him was barely visible.

Brodie was battered and bruised from being thrown around. It had become stuffy in the sack and he was lacking air. 'Can someone let me out now?'

Erin rolled the sack down around Brodie. He shrieked. The mist-spirits had suckered themselves to the windscreen of the van to make their vision even poorer. They started to launch jokes at them, a dozen at a time.

'What do you call a dear with no eyes, Erin?'

'No idea. Har, har, har, hee, hee.'

'What do you call a dear with no eyes and no legs, Erin?'

'Still no idea. Aaaaaggghhhhaaa, haa, haaa.'

The spirits held onto their stomachs as they laughed and guffawed their way through corny joke after corny joke and sang numerous out of tune songs. Some didn't even tell jokes – they just looked at one another and burst into bouts of sinful laughter. Brodie wasn't sure what was worse – the jokes, the singing or the ceaseless laughing.

'Move that stuff out of the way Erin,' he pleaded.

Erin looked at him, confused. 'What stuff?'

Brodie tapped on the window. 'Move this stuff out of the way, right now!'

Without delay, Erin responded to Brodie's desperate plea and wound the window down. Brodie screamed at the top of his voice, sounding like fifty bagpipes being blown at the same time. Harold swerved the van and ran up onto the misty verge. Erin tried shutting out the noise with her hands over her ears. Brodie continued his deafening scream until his own ears hurt.

There was a sound of popping corn as the mist-spirits

disappeared one by one. Brodie only stopped screaming when he ran out of breath and all of the spirits were gone. His throat was sore and his ears were ringing. 'They hate my screaming,' he croaked.

Some pairs of cautious eyes reappeared in the mist. Brodie screamed again and they disappeared in a few pops.

Harold chuckled as he steered the van back onto the road. 'Nice work Brodie. It will make driving easier with them out of the way.'

The mist thinned out and had finally disappeared as they drove on through Drumnadrochit. The night was crystal-clear and the Northern Lights pulsed gently through the Highland sky. Harold drove on in silence. Brodie watched his every move, unsure whether to trust him. He was ready to fight back if necessary.

'It will take the mist-spirits a bit longer to catch up,' Harold remarked eventually. 'They can move fast in the mist, but if they want to move the mist, it takes so much more energy and so much more time. They'll be on us soon. We've no time to lose. Gertruda will have us in sight now in her crystal ball, so she'll send her cronies after us.'

'How do you know so much? How come you can see all of this?'

'Yeah. How come you know so much?' Brodie chimed.

Harold chuckled heartily and removed his hand briefly from the steering wheel to ruffle the tufts of fur on Brodie's head.

Brodie scowled at him.

Harold eventually pulled the van into a deserted car park and wasted no time in getting Erin and Brodie out of the van. They followed him through his secret pathway and were soon descending the steps towards the small pebbly shore below Urquhart Castle.

'OK Brodie – now do your stuff. Sing for Nessie before the mist arrives,' said Harold with one hand on his hip and one hand beckoning out to the loch.

'If she'll come,' Brodie sighed deeply. 'The last thing she

said to me was that she would never do it again for a haggis – for any haggis. Anyway,' he grunted turning to the large butcher. 'How come you know so much?'

Harold beamed back at him. 'I was in Erin's position not so long ago,' he paused, counting back the years. 'Is Jock McHaggis a relation by any chance?'

Brodie gasped loudly.

'Your father then, I presume?'

Brodie nodded, his mouth still wide open. 'But …'

'Yes, your father was just as inquisitive as you. He arrived right here when I was fishing with my father. I took him home and we had some fun days, but I had to get him back. He didn't go to the forest, but Gertruda's cronies came looking for him. Unlike you, Brodie, he remained incognito. I managed to get him back home before Gertruda could find him. She had a gut feeling – a presence – but that was all. There was no proof that he was ever here. Ever since I waved your father off with Nessie, I've been back here nearly every night, longing to see him again. Longing to see Nessie again.'

'So you've always been able to see the other world?

'Fraid so,' he grunted to Erin. 'Not pretty at times. But yes, I refused to give up hope on the haggis and to keep my mind focussed, I took over my father's butcher business and have enjoyed keeping the traditional haggis myth alive – as a sort of duty.'

'How did you know that Brodie was here – with me?'

Harold Gunn smiled at Erin. 'Your neighbour, Mr Stewart, spoke of weird footprints up at that snowman that you built in the park. I went up for a look and my breath was taken from me when I realised that they were haggis footprints. Plus, with all of these goblins and boglouts running around looking for a haggis named Brodie McHaggis – that kind of gave it away too,' he laughed placing his hands on his well-fed stomach.

Erin laughed with him as she imagined the sight. Brodie giggled too before turning towards the water and clearing his nasal passages. He twisted his head around in a circle and snapped it back before sitting down. Lifting two of his three feet to his face, he began pumping his nostrils with his fingers, each squeeze and each movement along his nose giving a different, melodic note.

Erin loved Brodie's song. She had never heard anything so beautiful. A large lump formed in Harold's throat as he remembered Brodie's father doing the same thing all those years ago. Tears rolled from his eyes, down his ruddy cheeks and trickled over his chins before splashing onto his belly.

Brodie was oblivious to anything happening around him, as were Erin and Harold. His soft, angelic music turned the still, frosty night into something pleasantly haunting. When he finally stopped, he was exhausted. His eyelids fell down heavily over his eyes and he dropped his head between his shoulders, sighing deeply. How could his father have known all of this and not told him? If he had told him, then none of this would have happened. He started to feel anger towards his father.

Erin stepped forward and wrapped her arm around Brodie as they waited for Nessie to surface. He loved her warmth. He was going to miss her. Harold set his shovel-sized hand on Brodie's shoulder and they all waited in silence.

'Don't go yet, Brodie. We want to say goodbye!'

Brodie, Erin and Harold swung around and looked back up the steps towards the voices. Booger was running down them, followed by Gnogard and Ginny-ging. Brodie shrieked. His ears, eyes and fur stood tall as he reversed back into the water. Erin and Harold stepped in front of Brodie to protect him.

'No, no, no. We're friends – honest Brodie. We have to be quick – Gertruda can't find out that we've helped you,' Gnogard shouted as he skipped down the last few steps.

'Liar!' shouted Erin.

'But it's true,' he pleaded. 'How else do you think I got out of Gertruda's cottage? Booger left a way out for me.'

'I promise, all my work is good now,' Booger whined. 'Gertruda thinks I'm helping her – only I'm not. When you were in the cave, I sneaked up the stairs and removed the hex, momentarily, so that Gnogard could burrow out. I asked him to find Ginny-ging.'

'And I found her. Booger and me – we did it together. We got you out of the forest – with Ginny-ging's help.'

'It's true, Brodie. He knew that I could help you. Booger told him how Erin had helped me get energy from the diamond. Booger knew that my presence would weaken Gertruda and give you time to get out.' Ginny-ging flew down and perched on Erin's shoulder, smiling gratefully. 'Gnogard looked after my diamond.'

'Guarding that diamond has to be one of the most difficult things I've ever had to do,' said Gnogard through a wide grin, 'but it had its rewards. Think I've got a few more lady friends from it.' He winked at Erin and chuckled softly.

The ghillie dhu stepped closer. 'Please believe me. I'm going to find a new forest. I'm not an evil person any more. I'm really, really not. Really, I'm not. I love Brodie so much! '

Gnogard screwed his face up as he looked at the ghillie dhu. 'Aw shucks Booger, I wouldn't go as far as saying that. But, he's a good friend all the same. A really, really good friend.'

Booger reached his closed fist forward and beckoned to Erin to hold out her hand. Erin hesitantly stretched out her palm to accept whatever he was offering. The red piece of porcelain dropped into her hand. She gasped.

'How did you get it?'

Booger looked smug. 'Well, let's say that I may have sent Big Bag and Knobbly Knees on a mission that they thought they were doing for Gertruda.' He chuckled evilly. Even though Booger was a nicer ghillie dhu, he couldn't miss the opportunity to face evil with devilish behaviour.

'Now hurry. The mist is coming fast and Ly Erg will be with them.'

'Look!' shouted Erin. A dark silhouette of a witch on her broomstick raced across the loch. 'How did Gertruda get out?'

Ever the coward, Booger turned and ran back up the steps at the mention of Gertruda's name. 'Must go – can't let her find me.'

'So long Erin,' said Gnogard as he followed him. 'I'll keep in touch. So long Brodie – friend for life.'

Ginny-ging buzzed around Erin's head and brushed against her soft cheek. She smiled gratefully once more before zipping off into the night.

'That's not Gertruda,' Harold gruffed. It's the ravens.'

As the silhouette grew larger, Erin could see that it was made up of hundreds of black ravens. When she looked back to the steps, the mist-spirits were rolling down them. They looked like they were trapped in a bottle and pushing at the glass to get out as they forced the mist forward. Ly Erg stepped out from the mist.

'Erin – you have one final chance. Either you give me back my hand or you will be cursed by the Scotch Mist forever.'

Erin looked up at Harold Gunn. They had to get Brodie home first. They turned around to the loch and stood aghast. Brodie was nowhere to be seen.

CHAPTER TWENTY-ONE

Home, sweet home again

Brodie told his father everything that had happened. Jock McHaggis listened attentively, not once interrupting his son. It was the first time that he had actually listened to what Brodie had to say. He wished that he had taken the time to do it sooner.

'I'm sorry, Dad. I didn't know what was out there. I …'

'Son. It's my fault. I should have listened more. You can see why we tell nobody about it. It's too dangerous.'

Brodie nodded silently. He was no longer angry with his father. He was angry with himself. 'Who else knows?'

'Mirg McVey. Stan McGillis suspects something, but you can never … no, you *must never* tell a soul.' Jock's words were stern.

Brodie smiled at his father and for the first time, he felt a sense of responsibility. He wanted to forget everything – except Erin and Noremac, and maybe Booger and Gnogard.

Nessie had surfaced just as Harold and Erin had turned their backs to the loch and spoken to Booger and Gnogard. He nearly wept when he saw his father with Nessie. They begged him to come without letting the others know. It was too dangerous for Nessie. She didn't want Harold Gunn to see her. So Brodie had to leave without saying goodbye. Maybe that had been the best way. Goodbyes were too painful for him. He had left just after he heard how Booger and Gnogard had helped him escape from Gertruda's grips.

Brodie and his father tripled through the snowy heather back to Drumdrui, both deep in thought about what the future held. Could Gertruda still find a way to get to them?

***

Erin looked out across the water. 'He's gone!' she choked. 'We have to find him!'

'I think he's safe,' Harold sighed gently.

'How do you know?'

Harold kneeled down. 'Look – see this small oil slick floating on top of the water?' Harold dipped his hand in the water and rubbed the oil between his fingers as he sniffed at it.

Erin nodded slowly.

'It's from Nessie's skin. She's been here. I'd say that Brodie is safe.' Harold gazed out to the loch. He was disappointed that he hadn't seen her again – but he had been close to her. He stood up and placed his hand on Erin's shoulder. 'Now, I think you've got one very angry solider to sort out. I don't think that you want to live the rest of your life cursed by the Scotch Mist, do you?'

Erin tried to muster a smile as she turned back towards Ly Erg. The mist-spirits surrounded him as they all waited silently. Their eyes followed Erin's hand as she raised the piece of porcelain over Ly Erg's smouldering hand and set it into the hole. A red beam of light lit up the sky as the soldier's burnt hand glowed life into it once again. He turned to the mist-spirits and held up his red hand to them. They responded with a rapturous cheer. McCloud and Mildred swooped in and congratulated him personally. Charlie Boo rolled in and knocked them over like skittles. Laughing childishly, he zoomed around Erin and whizzed off into the mist. 'We're freeeeee and so is Brodie! Whoopee!'

Ly Erg addressed the mist-spirits. 'Brodie has gone. We have a reprieve.' He turned towards Erin. 'But if he ever comes back – just make sure he knows that we will all be waiting for him. We will be watching you as well – you are not so free.' Pivoting on his heel, the soldier marched up the steps and faded into the mist before he reached the top. The mist-spirits and the mist dissolved into the ground until the night was clear again.

Erin looked out to the loch. The ravens had turned around and headed back to the forest. She studied Harold as he gazed longingly across the loch. He must have spent the last thirty years hoping to see a haggis again. She knew that she too would be watching the loch daily as he had done – or still did. Although, she had more to remember Brodie by. She had pictures of him on her camcorder, and of Nessie. She had also recorded Brodie singing. Erin smiled at the fond memories. Then a wave of ice-cold dread washed over her.

'What is it Erin? You look … sick.'

Erin turned slowly towards Harold Gunn. 'I have recorded a lot about Brodie on my camcorder, including his story about where he lives, the Secret of Loch Ness and Nessie. There are even pictures of Nessie on it.'

Harold's smile widened. 'Excellent. Can you show them to me?'

Erin shook her head slowly and stared at him in a trance. 'It's in my rucksack, which is in the field just outside of the forest. I set it down to get the piece of Ly Erg's hand out of it and … well, we had to run and I forgot to pick it up.' Her voice drifted off as she continued to stare blankly at Harold. 'We have to get to it before anyone else does … before Gertruda finds it.'

Also Available:

The first in the Series

Brodie McHaggis and the Secret of Loch Ness

A fun-tastic adventure for all the family
Funny, full of suspense and truly magical

ISBN: 978-0-9551386-0-7

www.chloepublishing.com
www.brodiemchaggis.com